Gwendoline Riley was born in 1979. Her first novel, *Cold Water*, won a Betty Trask Award and was voted one of the top five first novels of 2002 by the *Guardian*.

Grubby
Manchester
continued ...

3/04

BY THE SAME AUTHOR

Cold Water

SICK NOTES

Gwendoline Riley

JONATHAN CAPE
LONDON

Published by Jonathan Cape 2004

2 4 6 8 10 9 7 5 3 1

First published in Great Britain in 2004 by
Jonathan Cape
Random House, 20 Vauxhall Bridge Road, London SW1V 2SA

Random House Australia (Pty) Limited
20 Alfred Street, Milsons Point, Sydney,
New South Wales 2061, Australia

Random House New Zealand Limited
18 Poland Road, Glenfield,
Auckland 10, New Zealand

Random House South Africa (Pty) Limited
Endulini, 5A Jubilee Road, Parktown 2193, South Africa

The Random House Group Limited Reg. No. 954009
www.randomhouse.co.uk

A CIP catalogue record for this book
is available from the British Library

ISBN 0-224-06429-0

Papers used by Random House are natural,
recyclable products made from wood grown in sustainable forests;
the manufacturing processes conform to the environmental regulations of
the country of origin

Typeset by Palimpsest Book Production Limited,
Polmont, Stirlingshire
Printed and bound in Great Britain by
Mackays of Chatham PLC, Chatham, Kent

She was born like it, I swear. I can see her howling herself rigid in her cradle. They are never happy, these sports which ordinary, humble people throw off: they belong nowhere and are insatiable.

Elizabeth Taylor, *Angel*

'Declare to whom? I want to know to whom?'

'To nobody, to everybody, to the first one who reads it. Why specify? To the whole world!'

'To the whole world? Bravo! And so there's no need for repentance; and not to any authorities!'

'No, no need, devil take the authorities! But write, if you're serious! . . .' Pyotr Stepanovich yelled hysterically.

'Wait! I want a face at the top with its tongue sticking out.'

'Ehh, nonsense!' Pyotr Stepanovich got furious. 'All that can be expressed without any drawing, just by the tone.'

Fyodor Dostoevsky, *Demons*

If you find one false excuse for yourself you will soon find a hundred, and be just what you were before.

When you really want love you will find it waiting for you.

Oscar Wilde, *De Profundis*

1

The bus moves slowly through the whirling sleet. The windscreen wipers switch slowly, dragging slushed snowflakes so cold water streams down constantly. I was one of just a handful of passengers boarding this late trip, but I walked right to the back to sit down and I folded my coat and scarf on the seat next to me to ensure I was left alone. And so I was.

I spent the journey – seven long hours up the motorway – trying to look through my reflection to catch the shrinking numbers on the blue signs, to see inside the cars with the flashing lights on the hard shoulder. And as the songs on my Walkman slowed I closed my eyes and must have rolled my head against the headrest trying to go to sleep, because loops of my hair have worked themselves loose of my ponytail. I can see in the window now how they have been snagged into peculiar orbits.

Rounding the corner on to Chorlton Street,

where Manchester's taller hotels and office buildings give way to the low canopies of the
terminus, our misted windows catch the weak
rising sun, and by degrees they flare, light up,
become entirely opaque. I take a hold of the
arms of my seat and breathe slowly. Because each
one is shining: perfect and blank.

I drag my suitcase across a pitted concourse
stuck with blackened chewing gum; it bangs
against bollards and down steps after me and I
can feel fear – something – rising in my chest
with the same dull thud. I see Donna – my
friend, my flatmate – waiting by the glowing
vending machines. Her dark hair is tucked away
in a yellow and black striped hat (my old hat,
actually) and she's letting her half-moon glasses
hang from her ears like a chinstrap, closing one
eye at a time to stare into a beige plastic cup
of something which she's evidently bought more
to warm her hands on than to drink. I stand in
front of her for a long minute before she notices
me looming there, slides her glasses up into place
and looks back.

The thing about me is – I'm double-jointed
in my left elbow, and so when I stand, as I often
do, as I'm doing now, with my hands jammed
in my hip pockets – one arm looks like it's

bending the wrong way. In summer, in short sleeves, the effect is more dramatic: the sheeny skin inside the joint stretches and shows up a lattice of red thread veins deep below. But even in a thick winter coat it's an unsettling trick, I know; jabbing a limb out at such an odd angle.

'Stop doing that with your arm,' Donna says now, and takes a hold of my elbow and clicks it around and back into place. 'You look disappointingly familiar,' she says.

'Don't be deceived,' I say. I pick up my case properly but make no move to leave. 'I have Tweetie-Pie and a Coca-Cola bottle tattooed on my ass.'

Donna leans back against the wall and twitches her eyebrows, her pale lips twitching too: a suppressed smile. 'On your what?' she says. 'Come on, car's this way.'

In the car I listen to the changing tones of the tyres on the wet roads, watching with one open eye the monochrome early morning suburbs scrolling by.

Donna says, 'So. The New World.'

And I say, 'White socks.'

She nods. The car is cold and it smells of her peppery perfume. Being only five feet tall she

3

has to sit on a cushion to see over the steering wheel.

By the time we get to Salford a chilly sunlight is hitting the clean snow crusts on the car bonnets and the bin lids. I can feel the brightness forcing itself in behind my eyes. Dew spangles the black twigs on the tree in front of our squat block. The path to our porch is frozen over. I lean on the front wall, thinking how to cross it, while Donna locks the car.

I've never smoked in my life; still, somehow, since I was a kid, I've had this habit of holding a phantom cigarette. While I'm thinking now I press two fingers to one side of my mouth and then swing them to one side, sighing out a stream of cold air and pinching my eyebrows together. There's no way around it. Even the strip of barren soil by the fence is glazed. I pick up my suitcase from by the gate and slide it across the bumpy tundra to the door. It spins slowly towards the step, making a thin, scratching sound. I set off after it, taking baby steps and holding my arms out: my red hands balled in tight fists; my eyes wide because all I can think is that at any moment I'll be slamming into the ground, with my knees, with my tail-bone. What I really feel like doing is getting down and crawling; that would surely be safest. Donna walks alongside carefully; the rubber soles of her tide-marked baseball shoes have more grip than these knee-high boots I've been wearing, with my jeans rolled halfway up my calves, with my twinset: my snowbound-Kansas 1957 look.

I sense I'm going to slip so I reach out and clutch Donna's scarf. I right myself okay but she sways.

'If you're going to fall *on your ass*, I think we should do this independently,' she says, looking round at me.

'Yes,' I say, and take hold of her coat sleeve; creak the stiff damp wool between my fingers. 'Independently while grabbing on to each other.'

I snap open my cardboard suitcase on my bedroom floor and find a tape amongst the tangle of jeans, dresses, cardigans. I click it into the player on the dresser and lie down on the bed with my hands behind my head and my coat and boots still on. Soon there's a timid tapping on the door; my green door which is gripped by the brass knuckles of a series of locks.

'Come in,' I say.

Donna pushes the door open but she doesn't come in. With her arms up and her feet apart she spiderwebs the doorway, looking in around this small room which she hasn't seen for three months. She's taken her coat off and I see she has some jack leads tied around the top of her jeans in place of a belt. She jerks her hipless middle side to side a couple of times so the plugs swing neatly.

'Sound tech. chic,' she says.

I raise my eyebrows but don't reply, just suck on a ratty snatch of my hair and resume staring into a corner of the ceiling. She climbs in now over towers of taped up cardboard boxes, from the time when I thought I might leave for good. Boxes I'm already narrowing my eyes at – because I don't intend to unpack them again. I flip over and lie on my front, and look at Donna with one eye while rubbing the other one. I feel very tired all of a sudden now I'm lying down. But Donna is staring at all the dusty empties over on the other side of the room; a couple of dozen, half-sized bottles, gin mainly, crowding at the end of the bed.

'They look like hungry baby birds,' she says, standing in a small patch of clear carpet and twitching her jack leads into pendulum motion again, in time with the slow music on my tape. 'Or those statues, those . . . I can't remember

6

. . . National Geographic . . . little clay people . . .'

'Yeah,' I say, sitting up. I turn the yeah into a yawn. I stretch my arms up and then pat my mouth. 'Yeah.'

'They've taken over. They're encroaching . . .'

Another nice yawn from me.

'Yes,' I say. 'It's very meta—' I lift the limp curtain to look out of the window at the bus stop.

'—phorical. Yes it is, Esther, yes it is,' she says.

'I bought you a present,' I say. 'It's on top of the case.'

She kneels down and retrieves a cheap snow globe from its tatty nest of tissue paper: a yellow cab and a cop car stupidly big next to warping plastic skyscrapers. She stays crouched there and nods as she turns it upside down a couple of times. But the cloudy liquid inside isn't viscous enough, so no matter how hard she shakes it the snow stuff falls too fast and is almost instantly back on the bottom; the sealed up scene as static and lifeless as before. She nods again and her black hair falls from behind her ears.

'Is that Ancoats?' she says. Then, 'You should clear them out.' She points at the bottles. 'Make room for the new ones at least.'

I blow on my cold hands.

7

'The heating's broken again,' she says. 'Do you need any shifts, by the way?'

I shake my head. Donna starts climbing out of the room.

'Cup of tea before I get off?'

I nod. 'Don't put any milk in,' I say.

I stop my music, get up and go down the hall to her room. On her door are two Polaroid photos I took of her years ago. In one she has her arms folded and looks bored beyond measure; in the other she's in close up, she's got red eye behind her glasses and she's growling fetchingly.

Donna has the same narrow bed and chipped nursery furniture as me but she's made more of an effort with her space. There's a duvet cover, framed postcards on the wall, ornaments even: dried up sea urchins, a crouching child figurine, a tiny pair of painted wooden clogs, a ship in a bottle and a Russian doll flanked by the two rubber ducks I got her for her last birthday. Also a plain brass photo frame holding a picture of a small girl standing by a piano. The kid's on tiptoe, reaching up to jab at the keys. The curtains behind her and the jumper underneath her dungarees are in sour seventies colours. Her facial expression is kind of sour too. That's Donna at her grandma's. A sardonic toddler, wouldn't you know it. I move her guitar, sit down on her unmade bed and look through the books on her pillow.

She comes and finds me and stands in the doorway with our tea. 'What are you on these days. Still your Westerns?' she says.

'No,' I say, 'I had to stop. I got tired of drinking tequila and living off beans and hotsauce.'

She nods.

'It wasn't such a healthy diet for me. Plus,' I lean forward to whisper, 'I got saddle sores.'

Donna rubs her non-existent behind and winces, then spins around slowly to bump down next to me.

'I'm reading a book called *Hunger*,' I say.

'What's that?'

'Well . . . how to explain . . . this man . . . he's hungry . . . then he eats and he's full . . . then he gets hungry again and he *doesn't eat* and he gets hungrier . . . then he sells his vest, and he eats. And he's full. That's the story so far.'

'Existential,' she says and grins to herself.

I flick up the collar on my coat then pull out the Biro I keep stuck in my ponytail. I make it a cigarette for one puff and then crunch it and wink. Donna turns up the collar of her shirt so

9

we match. Donna's got a great smile on account of her teeth: the front two on the top cross over one another. You can hear it when she talks, too; there are some consonants it sounds like she's kissing.

'I tried fasting a few weeks ago in pursuit of a transcendent experience,' I say, tapping my Biro over her mug.

'Okay,' she says. 'And? Did you see God?'

I shake my head slowly. 'No. Just black spots floating.'

I pick up the nearest book. A bath-read Jean Genet. I flick through looking for her annotations. There's just one I can find: a thin red line under the word 'trousers', a few pages in.

'More depravity,' I say.

She looks over my shoulder, at my stubby-nailed thumb tutting on the page.

'And you know when I was six,' she says, squinting, 'I got woodworm in my chuff from rubbing myself against library Ladybird books.'

She sighs and pulls her hair back out of her face.

'Don't look so aghast.'

'Aghast, well you know me, Donna, every time someone starts having sex with me I feel like phoning a psychiatrist.'

Sadly true. I start using the string attaching the tag to my teabag to floss under my nails. Donna shakes her head and leans right forward with her elbows on her knees. She huffs out a sigh.

'Esther, listen, I know you. You've just forgotten what it's like; what it's like to be with someone.' She jabs me with her elbow, but keeps looking straight ahead. I see I've started tapping all my fingers on the side of my mug. She keeps going, and bless her. 'You look at their eyebrow or their mouth or some hair in their ear, or their socks on the floor – if you're lucky – and you feel the way they feel and move, it's amazing. Don't you . . .'

I can't say I do. I reach across her to pick up another book, one of mine, I'm sure: Steinbeck, *The Red Pony*. I hold it up with a selling soap powder smile.

She clicks her fingers and nods and says, 'Now that's a sad book. This little boy starts shooting birds and stamping on ants. And all because his pony dies. And all he wanted to do was brush it and stroke it and love it. It's really a heart-breaking tale.'

'His pony,' I say.

But she doesn't flinch. She segues seamlessly

into a long and – let's not be churlish – enter-
taining story about twelve hours of true love
on a damp mattress, rolling around on spiky
toast crumbs, in a room with a non-functioning
gas fire and a nasty old maroon sheet drawing
pinned over a bay window.

'. . . and my arms were cold outside the
blanket, and the blanket *smelt of sick* . . .' – she
looks dreamy for a second, I swear – 'and there
were no curtains but the whole world felt warm
and buttered in this emotional haze.'

She swirls a small hand around to illustrate
the point. I don't mind Donna talking like this.
At least she does it with a certain *joie de vivre*.
But still. Enough. I rattle my Biro in my smile,
then put it back in my hair.

'I hate butter,' I say, karate chopping the edge
of the bedside table. 'I'm intolerant. And you
probably just had carbon monoxide poisoning.'

I stand up and point at her as I leave. 'You're
the enemy,' I say, then keep talking, walking
backwards down the hall to my room. 'You're
a propagandist! You've got no inner life!'

I lock my door, take my boots and coat off
and get in bed under my coverless duvet. I pull
it tight over my head: stare up at the soft cold
clouds it makes with a bare bulb on behind it.

Then see lava flows when I close my eyes.

Five minutes later I hear Donna leave, after calling in to tell me my tea is outside my door. I sit up and twitch the curtain to watch her edge down the path, get in her car and finally drive off to work. To a dingy café bar in town where she works the days and where I used to work the nights; on and off anyway. Our boss used to call us Cox and Box. But a lot of people just said Donna and Esther and it meant what it meant.

I have a stretch and a yawn and take my mug into the kitchen. The hallway smells hoovered and when I notice that it upsets me. I take a biscuit from the jar on the microwave but it tastes of nothing, and I'd feel glutted if I swallowed it, so I spit it out: leave a beige clod in the empty sink. I take my tea back to my room in a bad temper. I growl in the mirror. I'm not going to touch those boxes. Sitting on the bed, I lean back against the headrest and press my chin down on the faded denim on my knees. On the windowsill is a line of ancient tea-bag husks. I look at them for a while and smoke an invisible cigarette. A rank of cowering chrysalises. I'll tell Donna that one. I pinch and peel a couple of them off where they're stuck and toss them at the door, then I get up and sit cross-legged by my speakers. There aren't many records any more. I spent the week before I left off-loading my belongings. I sold all the songs I was sick of. And the ones too scratched for Vinyl Exchange to take; the ones with their cases cracked, their inlays torn or tea-stained, I threw them out. I did the same with three shoeboxes of dusty tapes, mostly stuff recorded off the radio when I was a teenager. It was October. I hip-hugged the bags I couldn't carry as I walked down the path to the bins.

Now I put on a song I haven't listened to in a long time. Still I find I recognise every soft in-breath, every squeak on the strings. It's a sad song which tells a sad story half-submerged. I can't tell what's happened, that's why I'll never get tired of it. But that's just three minutes some-thing then the drums go *sshh* ... the needle jerks up and the room is sucked into silence again. I sit still, curled up uncomfortably and feeling too aware of my breathing.

My first place – a bedsit I moved into when I was seventeen – was opposite a hospital in south Manchester. While I lived there I had a morbid habit of watching the comings and goings over the road. I used to stand stock still behind one curtain, or crouch down and just peep above the sill. It was six months before I realised there was never any need to hide. Because looking up and across, my small window was all but impenetrable, there was nothing to see but the pale reflections of the leaves on the trees in their car park: they flickered on a darkness.

After I saw that I could stare out with impunity: stand up and grip my elbow behind my back, or lean forward with my forehead sticking to the thick white gloss on the frame. I remember that broad sill, slathered with mossy slime around a puddle where the cats drank. It spread or it shrank, depending on the weather. I thought I was fine staying on there: I certainly never wanted to live with anyone, but Donna said I should move in with her, and — she was my friend — eventually I did. That was nearly two years ago. It's worked out okay. We both get on with our work: she writes her songs and, myself, I've got my notebooks.

I get back in bed and sleep most of the day. Each time I bob up into shivery consciousness I think, *Where am I?* then, *Damn*. At four o'clock I walk round to the off-licence, wearing a pair of Donna's shoes so I won't slip over. The sun's halfway down and the dying light is making all the red bricks look scarlet. On the way back I catch the eye of a kid sitting in the back of a small car stalled at the junction: belted in, staring out, he stares at me with no expression on his face. I look back and feel hollowed out in my stomach.

I spend the evening drinking in the kitchen chair. When Donna gets home there's a bottle in the bin, a mug in the sink, and me sprawled out on the tabletop. She mashes my hair and gets me a glass of water. I lift my head up and rest my chin in my palm. I spread my fingers over my face like the spines of a fan, but I'm being the opposite of a coquette: I stare out between where I'm holding myself up.

'I wish you'd been here on New Year's Eve,' she says, taking her coat and hat off, sitting down opposite me. 'It was a pathetic tragedy. I thought it would be cool to drink out of a pineapple. So I spent the afternoon in here, hollowing out this pineapple and laughing to myself. But I didn't realise that after two drinks it gets kind of water-logged and soggy.' Here she winces at her hands. 'So at the end of this party I was on these people's landing drinking beer out of this collapsed pineapple. I was all sticky. The next day everyone was saying, "What were you doing? You're disgusting. Where's your self-respect?" 'cause I was sick as well. Sick all down myself.'

She rolls her eyes at me.

'I get the picture.'

I sigh and stare at her. Her eyebrows are half raised. Her nose is still red.

Looking down at my left hand I see I've written on it in Biro: DON'T GO OUT. I can't remember doing it. Donna points at my face and I reach behind me to get a saucepan off the rack. I see my reflection in the base, and my sentiment echoed in a pale print on my right cheek.

'You should come out. People have been asking after you today,' she says.

I watch myself yawn: the webby black drool dried on my cheek creases and cracks.

'Tomorrow, maybe,' I say. I frown. 'What day is it tomorrow anyway, Donna?'

2

It's Tuesday. And at 5 a.m. I've been up for over an hour, walking round the three square feet of bare carpet in this bedroom, lying down there, too, with my knees bent and my tea mug on my chest. It's taking forever for the sun to come up.

I stand at the window. Through the frost-feathers on the cold pane I watch the traffic on Trinity Way: the smoky breath of the exhausts, the blinking indicators, the staring tail lights. Windblown rain hangs a murky gauze around the dim streetlights but still, it would take too much effort to convince myself to stay in. I put on most of my clothes – my twinset over a T-shirt, my wool coat, three pairs of socks pulled up under my jeans – I zip up my boots, take a Biro from the mugful on my dresser, stab it in my ponytail and head out.

Pulling my musty grey scarf up over my head I cross the main road and start walking fast: clashing through leaden gutter puddles, slamming my boots on to the grit. The cold bores into my ears and the raw air I'm breathing hurts my chest.

On the empty bus into town there's a window that won't shut. I sit near the front but I can still feel the sharp cold on the back of my neck, insinuating itself between the windings of my scarf. I sit with my knees up and my arms crossed. A watery sunrise starts to gasp through between the buildings.

I walk up to my old favourite café, on Piccadilly Approach. It smells of Dettol and sausages and wet white bread. Three men in heavy fluorescent coats and skip caps are sitting around one table sawing up bacon and reading their papers. I'm writing in my detective note-book and drinking black tea when two old-timers come in. The tall one swings an elbow into his dazed friend's ribs while they stand by the greased chrome counter.

He says, 'Look at her. Writing your will out, are you?'

I raise my eyebrows and tap my cold nose with my pen. In fact I'm trying to write about my mum.

She left my dad when I was three and my

brother not yet walking. While he was at work one day she took us across the Mersey from Liverpool to her dad's house on the Wirral. She made several trips that day, transferring all her things, thirty years unedited accumulation, back to the room where she grew up. We stayed on there, so – isn't life funny – I ended up going to the same schools that had made her miserable. Another irony – she escaped from my dad pushing her around, but brought my brother with her: a time bomb, buckled in the baby seat.

We lived with her gruff dad for five defeated years before he died and we moved. Just up the road, but we moved. When we'd been in our house a couple of years my mum got the builders in to divide the large living room into two: one for us kids, one for her to keep nice and entertain in, or, as it turned out, one for my brother and his friends to play Nintendo in, one for her to hide in and watch TV.

It was around that time I started having my nightmares. I was scared to go to bed so I'd sit on the end of the settee in her living room, reading, while she stretched out and watched the soaps and the films after. When she'd gone up I'd stay in there with the big light on and read until morning. She took me to see a doctor about that. I was on mild sleeping pills for a short while, then all through that winter I was sent to counselling at Bebington civic centre: a flat, pebble-dashed complex, with a doctor's, a library, a police station, all in boxy buildings whose windows were portholes.

I took the shortcut there after school, across the frozen playing fields. There was some kid's porn stash, torn up and bloating in a rain-filled tyre track. There were always oversized black-birds on the falling-over goalposts. I stamped over grass that cracked under foot and scoured the skin off my knees and hands more than once. When my teacher saw me with those scabs she said, 'You should get some hobnails fitted.'

I had my sessions in a small room next to the surgery. A non-intimidating room: there was a huge, low chair for me and posters of animals on the green chalk-coloured walls: grumpy muddy hippos, baby monkeys with their rope-thin arms around each other. There were biscuits. Cardigans were worn. I spent hours and hours in there but I remember nearly none of what was talked about. Just that at the end of my first visit, as I was reaching under my chair for my coat, the man I'd been listening to leant forward with his big eyes shining, and said,

'You know what one of the best things about being a grown-up is?'

I shook my head.

'You get to eat your pudding first!' He grinned at me and drummed his fingers on his knees. 'When I first moved out to university I loved that,' he said. 'I was in the supermarket once and there was a little boy standing up in a trolley by the fridges and I just picked up this yoghurt and I said – I get to eat this before my dinner if I want!'

Every time I saw him from then on I imagined him with yoghurt all over his face.

I was also enrolled in activities to get rid of my excess energy. So I had brief stints at trampolining, swimming, indoor tennis, archery. For a while I took ballet classes, in a dank talcum-smelling church hall. That ended when one week my mum came to get me and was told it would be best if I didn't come back. Asking why, the door to the changing room was duly opened and as she tells it I was lying down in there and rolling along the floor and back again, had been doing so since I arrived. It sounds plausible. I told Donna about it recently, and she said, 'Well, you were just expressing yourself.'

But that's our excuse for everything. When I

was on a downswing last year and kept pissing on my bedroom carpet – like an angry cat, Donna said, rolling her eyes – I was 'just expressing myself'. And when I saw her spitting in my ex-boyfriend Richard's whisky, it was the same thing. I wonder how long it will wash. Still, I'd find it surreal to live otherwise.

My mum, my brother and I went on our only holiday when I was ten. The poor woman used her hard-earned cash to have us stranded together in some misery pit in Spain. Just once during that fortnight I covered myself in chalky factor 60 and braved the pool, when it was empty in the evening. I lay on my front on my brother's lilo. I had hold of the sides and I was rolling it about, almost tipping over. I think maybe I was toying with death.

At someone's suggestion I spent the last two weeks of the wet summer before I started Wirral Girls Grammar in a modern boarding school down South. My brother's friends had been round every day of the holidays, while my mum was at work. I didn't like being there when they were in anyway. They had the run of the place.

I packed a week in advance. The bottom of my small suitcase was lined with all my different coloured socks: fourteen pairs, laid out next to each other. Quite perverse of me, because I knew I'd end up wearing the red pair more than once. That was a given. I'd also taken some mascara from my mum's room. She had three decades worth of cosmetics in compartmentalised dusty plastic trays in her dresser drawers: grey sponges turning to powder, bottles of orangey chalky goop, lipstick stumps. She'd brought it all back with her when she left my dad. I'm a redhead like him, but my eyelashes are blonde, and they fan down bluntly. I'd got self-conscious about it all of a sudden and started using some of my mum's dry old mascara. I applied it every morning. Sometimes I would spit on toilet paper to rub it away at night, sometimes I just picked out the larger coaly lumps; mostly I let it accrete until bath day, or until I had a tantrum.

Before she dropped me off my mum took me for lunch in a huge chain pub. We sat on damp benches in the beer garden. I ordered vegetarian lasagne. It came with chips and peas. I didn't eat much of it. I had two glasses of Coke, though, which ordinarily I wasn't allowed, especially during holidays, because then she said, and quite rightly, I would 'spoil things for everyone'. While I drank it I pressed my left hand against the table, turning my elbow inside out and back again over and over, and read a book I had open on my knee.

'You'll get indigestion,' Mum said.

This school was a two-storey red-brick building forming three sides of a courtyard. There were two dormitory blocks and half a dozen mobile classrooms near some sparse, off-limits woods. Us kids had lessons in astrophysics, zoology, Jacobethan tragedy. And that was *before* we broke for coffee. All those teachers in T-shirts kept telling me I was very quiet, wasn't I? I nodded at them.

At mealtimes we carried our food in moulded trays to large round tables. We poured glasses of squash from a huge jug. It was unwieldy, losing its centre of gravity in those small hands and short arms, so the drink was always sloshing out, sticking the paper cloth to the Formica then dripping over the table lip into our laps. Whenever I spilt I heard my mum saying, 'You've never understood liquids, have you?'

At the end of the first week there was a disco in the main hall. Evidently I was keen to avoid this. I walked straight back to the dormitories after my classes. No one noticed me go. I went to the one unoccupied room at the end of the girls' corridor. It was the same as the room I'd been sleeping in. Behind the six beds was a row of fitted wardrobes. Their doors were on slippy tracks: a nudge and they slid open with no sound; anything else would send them slamming back and forward. Inside smelt of sawdust and glue, along with that smell which comes from frequent hoovering, familiar to me from the school library. It figured because there was carpet inside the cupboards, on the walls as well as the floor. There were blankets folded on the top shelves. I waited in there until dinner was finished then I went to the dusty window and watched everyone coming out.

There were groups of kids criss-crossing the boggy lawn. There was one girl I had noticed before. She was walking up and down a low wall. Each time she lost her footing her outstretched arms twitched. On an impulse I licked the glass. The dust was so thick I didn't lift it, but left tiny bubbles sitting on the stripe of the smear trail. I rubbed it with the bottom of my T-shirt and stared out more. It got darker by degrees in there and I could feel the ceiling shadows start to crawl behind me. I smoked my invisible cigarette and watched for a while, then I pushed open the window as far as the safety latch would allow and called to her. She looked up and frowned, then she saw me, and came inside and found me.

Donna with the lazy eye. She'd been brought down from Manchester. Her black hair was short at the back with a blunt fringe. The T-shirt she was wearing that day was orange. It said *International Sports Society* and had a silhouette of a man with a javelin. Mine had cartoons of a croissant and a bicycle. The things they do to kids. She's two years older than me, so she was thirteen then, but she looked much younger, acted it too. Years later she told me that even then she was regularly sent home from school swinging her knickers in a plastic bag. We waited together and watched until everyone else had disappeared. Then we went and sat under the low child-sized sinks in the bathroom, because Donna liked the sound when you turned all the taps on with no plugs in. I did find I could imagine anything while listening to that noise. Beyond that I have less than no clue what we talked about. Neither has she. It got late and we heard tired footsteps dragging up the stairs. We went and sat in the wardrobe in the empty room.

I woke up first and stretched my stiff legs in front

of me. I couldn't hear any people awake next door. No one was fussing in the corridor, there was just the shush of rain on the window. I slid open the wardrobe door and crawled out, then stood up. The light at the wavy top and bottom of the nubby wool curtain was that strange ethereal blush that can mean any time of day. I clacked the rings along the rail and let light run in across the six neatly made beds.

Trees shuddered thickly behind the tinted glass. It looked tropical: the near silent sheets of rain, the dripping foliage, but I was freezing, my toes were grey with the cold. I stepped back into the wardrobe and pulled my blanket back around myself. I watched a cloud shadow move over the carpeted walls and bend in the corners of the ceiling, folding over the ridges of the architrave. I rolled my head to look at Donna. I said:

'You're staring at me.'

Staring with serious sleepy eyes. Her face looked soft and swollen with sleep. There was a map of blanket creases all over one cheek. She pulled a pale thin arm out of her cocoon and pointed at me for a second.

'You've got all black round your eyes,' she said.

'Oh,' I rubbed one eye with two fingers, 'I know.'

She did the same.

'If I rub my eye do I get black?' she said, and kept rubbing.

I suppose it would be cute to say that I gave her a drag on my phantom cigarette then, but things aren't like that between us at all.

My mum said she'd buy me a watch for going to senior school so I chose one from the catalogue. It had scratchy stylised drawings of two giraffes and a zebra on the face, and a thick elastic strap: red with brown and cream zigzags. She tapped on my door early on the Saturday. I'd already been up for a while, had opened my window because I could smell the eggs she was frying for my brother's breakfast, and I hated that smell. The rain was spitting in on my arms and on my book. I told her I was coming and she went to wait in the car.

As we walked through the dark corridors of Birkenhead Pyramids shopping centre I looked down at the gritty puddles swirling over the cracked yellow concrete, the cigarette ends swollen in the grids, a squashed chip on the side of my shoe.

'What's the matter with you?' my mum said. 'Take that face off. I've only come out for you.'

I shrugged and looked up and around instead.

I put my watch on as soon as she'd paid for it. I adjusted the time as we walked back to the car. We stopped at the new drive-thru place on the way home because my mum had said she'd get my brother a couple of burgers and a milk-shake.

'Do you want anything?' she asked me, looking across, but I was absorbed with my watch and just shook my head slowly.

A few weeks later, I was standing on the back step in my school skirt and the T-shirt I'd slept in, chewing an apple for breakfast. My brother was in his living room with the TV on. I could hear shrill laughter and music, even through two shut doors. I could hear my mum's high-pitched humming in the kitchen, too, while she made him his eggs before she went to work. Then that stopped and her head came through the back window.

'Do you want any hot food while I'm doing your brother's?'

I shook my head and lifted up my half-eaten apple and wiggled it.

She nodded then said, 'Where's your watch gone, Esther?'

'It's in my bag,' I said.

'Well, put it on, you'll lose it if you don't wear it. Let me see you do it, or you'll forget.' She pulled an anxious face and didn't go back to her cooking. She stayed at the window.

'I will,' I said. 'I'm eating.'

I walked past her with my eyes down and went upstairs to finish getting dressed. I came back with my watch in my grey cardigan pocket.

'Where's that watch, Esther?' she said. 'That was a good watch to last you.'

I started putting it on. Then said, 'Don't make me wear it.'

I spoke very quietly, and wouldn't look her in the eyes. I just stared at a tea towel on a hook behind her.

'Oh for God's sake. What's wrong with you?'

My mum's voice went up. She shook me by the shoulders and I went limp instantly.

'Get up,' she said.

We could hear the tinned tomatoes hissing in the pan, could smell them burning.

'You liked that watch last week. What's changed?'

No reply from me.

'What's changed, Esther? Has someone said something at school? Come on, wear it. Come on. Come on, wear it. What's happened?'

I covered my eyes with my wrists. I sunk against the tiled kitchen wall and hid my face with my fists, pinched my shoulders forward, crushed my legs together at the knees. I held myself braced, feeling my cheeks getting hot and itchy where the colour was spreading. I was blubbing bubbles from lips all glossy and slick with spit. Then I was crying and making no noise at all, searching for a sound to let out. I took a long indrawn breath, felt a twinge in my sinuses. I blinked wetly and felt tears dripping from the corners of my eyes down on to my neck and ears.

'What's happened, Esther?' she kept saying.

'Nothing,' I said, sniffing. It was true. But my face was worn out with crying, like a baby's.

'Well, what's all this for? For God's sake,' she said. She was pulling a harried face. 'Go and get cleaned up. I'm going to be late now. For God's sake. You're supposed to be bright. You act like someone's abusing you.'

But I felt calm all of a sudden. I even yawned a bit, while I wiped my red eyes with the back of my hand.

My mum always asked me, 'Why's everything so traumatic?' A fair question, but it was a difficult feeling to describe: that something in me was struggling, clawing at a coffin lid. Then I'd start to feel like a holy statue with the tears running down. When I used to cry around Donna I'd say, 'I'm so alone' over and over. She'd never say 'But you've got me', she'd say, 'Everyone's alone. What are you talking about?' That's as good a reason as any why we're friends.

As I've said: my mum never could throw anything away. Occasionally there were manic Sunday cleaning sessions, though. These started with her thudding the Hoover against my bedroom door in the small hours and ended with her coughing in the cupboard under the stairs while she transferred dusty tinsel and undrinkable duty-free liquors from old cardboard boxes to newer ones. By midweek things would look much the same. There were always unruly piles of papers paving every corner of every room, and plastic crates, these beige plastic crates, that climbed the stairs, colonised the living rooms. They were cracked and dusty and gummy on the bottom (if you ever saw the bottom, having had cause to rifle through newspaper pull-outs, obsolete guarantees, years old cut out food coupons, dead batteries, empty pens, pink and grey striped chemist's paper bags she was saving). The only place she couldn't clean was my brother's living room. She tried to go in and collect mugs from there one evening and he came at her with the occasional table, stabbing the legs at her chest. I was standing in the hallway. I heard his friends laugh. So, that room never got done; anyway, suffice to say, that house contained a lot of rubbish.

One afternoon when I was skipping school I was making myself a cup of tea and I threw out a carton of sour milk. While the fridge door was open I found myself going through all the shelves in there, dropping jars of furry jam, a cracked block of cheese, my brother's half-finished turkey steak (that she'd put in a Jiffy bag a week ago) into the bin too. I emptied the rotting contents of a stack of plastic tubs, and then from one cupboard I threw out a dozen empty jam jars, a box of pellet-dry raisins and a bag of grub-infested flour. I lifted the liner out of the bin and took it upstairs to clean out the crammed, talc-smeared bathroom cabinet while I was at it. The clacking jars stretched out the bottom of the thin bag. When it was full I tied it up and put it by the front door.

I went into my mum's living room with my book. I'd picked the lock with one blade of a pair of scissors when I heard her get home from work at around six. I went out to say hello.

She put her work bag on the kitchen stool, filled the kettle, opened the fridge.

'What have you done – where's all the food?' she said.

'I threw out some chutney,' I said.

'No you didn't, what have you thrown out now? What have you done?'

She went and got the bin bag from by the front door. Her face was red and her mouth kept turning down at the corners.

My brother came and stood in the kitchen doorway.

'She's thrown my cards away, too,' he said.

Which honestly wasn't true.

'What cards, playing cards?' she said.

'Football cards. Bruce Grobbelaar's missing, they were on the windowsill in my living room.'

'Why have you done that, Esther?' she said. 'You are spiteful.'

She crouched down by the bag and started picking through it. She found one of the toilet detergent-block cases I'd put in there.

'This is re-usable,' she said and put it beside her on the lino where she was now sitting, back on her haunches with her winter coat spread around her.

'You had six of them,' I said.

'They're all different makes,' she said and lifted the neck of the bag so she could look in. She took out another one, a scummy pale green basket, and put it next to her. 'What else have you thrown out? Tell me. Why do you always have to make more work for me?'

'Have you found my cards, Mum?' my brother said. He was still standing in the doorway, breathing heavily.

My mum put her arms deeper in the bin bag and looked up at me. I could smell the rotten food: a dry smell and a slimy smell together.

So, you tell me, would it be worse if I were to leave her there on the kitchen floor, picking through rubbish, on her knees like that meek ornament girl on Donna's dresser, or worse if I were to take the bag and force my way through the sliding doors, past my brother's slamming shoulders, to take it upstairs and empty it out on her bed? So she can find whatever it is she wants so badly? Which of them is worse? Really?

I mean, in fact I did the second thing. And my brother gave me a good kicking for it when my mum started crying, so we were all quits. For that night at least. From my locked room, later, I heard those two stage-whispering about me on the landing.

Not that it means anything, but I did always go and say I was sorry after. And it really was wholly pointless because it never was acknowledged as anything other than a signal for a blank-eyed diatribe from her. She wasn't talking to me at all, just spooling out a loop of sing-song rhetoric: why-oh-why, what's wrong with you etcetera. I came out of this woman's stomach supposedly and she looked through me talking on and on. The thing about me now is — I just can't endure conversations which aren't conversations. I won't have any part of that. It made me panic when she went off like that but, really, I don't know what I wanted from her. She was more miserable than I could imagine, I know that now. I knew it then, vaguely, which is why I didn't care what I did. I thought that whoever she really was wasn't who she was living as. The real person, it seemed to me, was in there somewhere, but was safe in a beatific idiot-sleep, while this simulation she'd had to throw up at some point worked all day and watched TV and hoarded things and shredded up evenings nagging and crying.

I stayed away from school for the best part of my final two years, writing myself sick notes and meeting Donna in Liverpool or Manchester, or else saying yes to my name at registration, then going to the toilets with a book and staying there. I'd lock the door, take my shoes off and put my feet on the hot pipe. I'd read and feel so peaceful. Sometimes I spun the taps on in all the sinks. It's true about the running water. You can hear anything you want to in it. I left at sixteen with no qualifications whatsoever. My mum clawed her face for months afterwards, you can imagine. I wasn't supposed to be swabbing tables for a living. But that's a life lesson she never learnt: leave the things that make you lonely. At all costs, leave. It's obvious. She left my dad for her dad and brought us with her. Mistake. You can buy into absurd situations if you don't think just twice. I don't know why people are so keen to freefall into that kind of fiction.

I've not spoken to my mum in a few years now, but oddly enough last night her mobile kept phoning me of its own accord, so I got to eaves-drop on her evening until it cut out. I could hear the contents of her handbag rattling – maybe muffled a little by all the used but *re-usable* tissues balled up in there – with each step. Each trudging step. I could hear Mark – that's her new husband – talking endlessly and her making breathless laughing noises while her shuddery, catching-up walk was enacted perfectly by the tick-tock bumping of the bag. They must have been walking home from the pub. I kept listening. I didn't hang up. I could hear her walking and walking and him cheerily speechifying up ahead.

I didn't go to the wedding. I went for a meal with the pair of them in Liverpool a few weeks beforehand and that was enough. I was on time for this lunch, but they seemed to have been in the restaurant for a while; sitting together on one side of a table and sharing the menu. They both smiled up at me at the same time. Two stretched smiles. I bumped down on the bench opposite them and smiled back.

Mark is a loud, baggy-eyed fellow my mum met at one of her groups. During the meal she kept saying things to him like: 'You never do wear that shirt,' and then pouting and looking at me.

She had asked me if I'd read at their wedding. But while we were all staring into our soup she said:

'Oh, you don't need to read anything out anymore. *Mark* didn't like what I'd chosen.'

Then she looked at him with a pouty hurt look on her face, primping her mouth. She was wearing her hair down, she kept tucking it behind her ears and then pulling it forward again.

He waved his spoon about and said, 'Well, that was just doggerel, what you showed me. It was greeting card verse.'

My mum made her face some more and looked at me, then some squeaky hurt noises until he put his hand on her neck and said, 'Shush, shush.'

I kept looking outside and the rain was coming down.

There was a mistake with my mum's main course. When she told the waiter he started talking down to her as though she'd read the menu wrong. He was very young and very mean. My mum's voice started to rise in pursuit of assertiveness, self-possession, other words she's read about. Her voice got thinner as it got higher.

Mark put his elbows on the table and his hands over his ears. He squeezed his eyes shut. All the deep lines on his face were drawn into those scrunched up eyes. He's one of these people who hates scenes, as it turns out. Which is fair enough; who doesn't? He was crunching his face up so hard that this iridescent purplish-ness, this nacreous mussel-shell sheen, developed on the strained, shattered skin. He stayed like that until the waiter had gone. For her part my mum was breathing in tiny breaths. When the right food was duly brought out, her hands shook when she picked up the knife and fork. And I knew what that waiter would be saying about her as soon as the kitchen door swooped shut after him. I heard it close and I knew what words he'd be using. I couldn't stand it.

When my mum put her glasses on to read the dessert menu she looked up at Mark with her eyes big and blinking there, her chin nudging up. He patted her hand and she went back to choosing her pudding. I thought I could see their whole life together in that gesture, bickering all day, baby-talking in the dark between the days. It's only depressing because I feel like making it depressing. I don't know why I'm remembering all this, deliberately beating this path backwards. I'm being as bad as her with her nose in that bin bag, poking around, I know I am, but I can't seem to help myself.

Mark doesn't bully her, so that's something, because that's been her life so far, with her dad, with my dad, with my brother. Yes, I know I was a monster to her as well, but – how to put this? – at least I cross my legs when I sit down. Is that crass? I'm going to suck down some tea, look out of this window and think about that.

3

I put my pen back in my ponytail and walk down to Oldham Street to see Donna in work. On the chalkboard outside the café – the point illustrated with cartoon faces:

DONNA'S MAGIC COFFEE – *turns your mouth upside down* . . . is slowly being washed away by the listless rain. My eyes ache from the harsh light edging the dark clouds. I want to be inside, to slouch in soft gloom for a while.

Donna has put on an old pair of fancy dress fairy wings: a relic from a long ago party. There are a dozen holes stretching in greying nylon pulled over a bent wire frame. The wing tips trail ribbons and bells, the glitter on them looks greenish. When she sees me she mimes pouring two bottles into her mouth, then crosses her eyes and staggers about, this way then that way. She's on a dim deck in a fuzzy storm. Donna as a Vigo movie. I click on the fan at the end of the bar. I say:

'Wind machine.'

The blades speed up in their cage. I sit down and watch the rainbow playing inside the bars; the sheen on the spinning dust. Donna puts the coffee grinder on and starts drawing several spirits into two red mugs. A curly-haired sad sack sitting by the window looks up from his glass.

'Alcoholic witches,' he says.

I turn my head slowly to hiss at him and he starts muttering, 'Ever since I was at school . . . bloody domineering women . . . standing in the pulpit, saying . . . eat your cabbage . . . maybe that's why I'm like what I'm like . . .'

Looking past him I see someone outside in an enormous, filthy anorak, no face visible, just two tapering grease-glossed sheets of hair curving out of a fur-lined hood. He moves slowly past the smoked-glass picture window.

'Donna,' I say, slapping my hand on the bar, 'an *Eskimo* just walked past – I swear to God.'

Donna looks up and nods, says, 'Well, this is a city of extremes . . .'

I take my drink to one of the empty tables near the back of the room; lean back then lay back on it. I feel its viscid surface velcroing my coat. I lie completely still, with my mug on my chest, listening to my breathing and staring up at a tight tangle of wires falling through a hole in the patchy plaster. A sickly yellow glows in two enormous, leaded glass light shades which hang askew on gold chains. I look at them too long. When I swing my legs down and stand up darkness falls in around burning shapes and I have to blink and blink to make Donna more than a silhouette. Then I go and sit back at the bar to read the papers and harangue her.

'Donna, I'm bored to death,' I keep saying. I'm waiting for her to snap and shout at me but she doesn't.

'Well, the new Saturday girl's just called to say she's coming in to get her wages,' she says. 'Scottish Mary. You'll have to tell me what you think of her.'

She twitches her mouth then flutters off to do some wiping.

I don't know what Donna was expecting, but as it turns out I talk to Mary for less than five minutes before I decide I'm going to need a poster of her for my bedroom wall. She comes in sighing and sits up at the bar next to me. She's very tall and very young looking. She's got a greying fabric lily in her dark, bobbed hair. Donna introduces us. I say, Hey there and she

44

looks at me and nods. She takes a note out of the plastic bag of fivers and change Donna's just thrown her and gets herself a brandy. She offers me and Donna one too, circling a finger around and raising an eyebrow. Donna gets the drinks then asks Mary how her Saturday night went. Something must have gone down, Mary just rolls her eyes. She tells us both about her evening, her duff date. She talks quickly but doesn't jabber, and then suddenly she slows down and catches your eye. I'm hypnotised. So is Donna. I know because I'm watching her too.

'Sweet Jesus,' Mary says, 'I don't think I have high standards, I just want someone to entertain me for half an hour or so with conversa-tion, and they're *always* a fucking disappointment. So this is why I decided I didn't want to talk to them. I didn't want to know their stupid names.

'That worked for a while but now I'm getting caught out again. My feminist politics have been making me *angry*, because I catch these boys giving me a look like I'm some Godless slat-tern they can disapprove of . . . I think: *I don't like that look*. I think: *Fuckers.*'

Here she widens her eyes slowly and then bangs a fist on the bar. I bounce in my stool in

45

concert with the cups in their saucers and the tin ashtray there. I'm getting carried away.

'But it's okay,' she says, and turns to stare at me, 'because they don't get to stick around.'

She stands up and shakes her hair over her coat collar, then she fixes us both in turn with a look and says this, the clincher: 'Make them lick your fanny, then kick them out in the gutter.'

The snouty, scuffed green camera case she puts her money and tobacco tin back in bumps on her backside as she leaves, *bam-bam-bam*, it goes, then she stops in the doorway to snap up one slack Argyll sock, and she's off again, past the window: her flared knee-length skirt twitching one way, then the other.

Donna takes off her glasses and rubs them on her sleeve.

'Wow, she must be six feet tall at least,' I say.

Donna nods. She says, 'When we were working together last week I kept running past her at ribcage height and I thought, Isn't nature diverse?'

I drink one more magic coffee and then I feel itchy to be out in the cold again.

All that caffeine makes my heartbeat tremulous.

As I walk I'm nodding to myself and running my tongue over my tapping teeth, which all of a sudden feel like they're made of polystyrene: strangely squeezable, and creaky. My fingers are chewing the coins in my coat pockets as I plough on through the curdled snow lumps in the gutter, avoiding the pavements with their polished crust of pockmarked ice.

I stop in Chinatown to buy some cheap shoes, embroidered velvet Mary Jane slippers. Now my feet are freezing but at least I can stay upright. I swing my boots in circles as I walk. When I pass the Odeon a clutch of kids are coming out and blinking in the daylight, such as it is. Kids with harried parents. They yap out new enthusiasms to mums and dads who are nodding while they try and get their hats and gloves back on them, tug their arms through anorak sleeves. I see a boy with his dad. Both in jeans and desert boots and fluorescent ski coats. He keeps his gloved hand on the little boy's head while the kid acts out a fight scene. He has his hand in the boy's dark hair – a ball and a claw – and he keeps laughing and the kid keeps flapping his fists. It's happening slowly because I'm hot in the head from that coffee. All I can hear is the white noise of the rain on the road. It would be nice to chop Dad's rigid arm so the kid could run off. But he wouldn't, would he? That's the thing: he'd stay around like he was tethered on a string, dodging back, hanging back, but following. Kids don't like me anyway. I have to sit down. I crouch against the wall, under the film posters, and lean forward to breathe between my knees.

Back in the flat the bathroom is spinning so I spin the opposite way, smashing both my elbows on the tiles. Then I fall on my knees and make woozy eyes at myself inside the bottom half of the looming mirror. I start sweet-talking my smeary reflection in a sibilant whisper, twitching one eyebrow up and nodding. I get bored with that, rock forward on to all fours and crawl off slippily down the dark hallway towards my bedroom, grazing my knees through my jeans as I go. My eyes are stinging and my skin has an electric tingle in the cold. Silence presses in to my thoughts: where I'm making a sententious speech to someone I knew once. I sit down with my back against the radiator. I feel the burn of the cold metal through my cardigan. I hold a hand out and see myself blurring around the edges. Well . . . either blurring or glowing.

That's quite the question. Who knows what I'm playing at? Debonair self-sabotage I wish. More like shaking a broken clock and then listening if it's started ticking again. I stand up and shake myself, clench my teeth to make myself calm. Then I go into the kitchen, take some of my donated crockery from the cupboard and start bowling it down the hallway. I wear myself out at that, and decide to make a nice ghoulish suburban scene for when Donna comes home. I crouch in a darkling corner, with my shoulders hunched, my knees drawn up and a faraway look in my eyes. Broken china round my bare feet.

'I have missed you,' she says when she gets in and finds me.

I feel a lot better. I don't hoover now, I just put my shoes back on and pick up the bigger plate shards, then find a black marker pen in the cutlery drawer and write on a sheet of our thick, cream paper:

BARE FEET BEWARE

and lay it by the front door with the snow globe holding it in place.

★

49

I put some vegetables in a pan and sit on the kitchen counter reading my book. Donna points at the Chinese symbols embroidered in blue on the toes of my damp new shoes.

'What do they mean?' she says

I lift my feet up one by one and say, 'Well, Left and Right, obviously.'

'Love and Peace,' she says.

She comedy winces. I comedy shudder.

While we're eating Donna says: 'Did I ever tell you about my old friend Seymour?'

I shake my head.

'I know him from years back, before you moved in. Someone came in today and told me he's been put away because he tried to kill himself. He took all kinds of pills, apparently, then went and sat in an afternoon show in the Odeon, some romantic comedy, hoping to slip away. This was the plan. But I guess the film was really bad' – here she does a sideways look, an eyebrow twitch – 'because he left and he was found wandering around Piccadilly Gardens.'

She shakes her head. I think about the story. I nod. Then I chip in.

'I remember a *Crimewatch* story about a woman who disappeared. They had CCTV footage of her walking away with this man, down the high street, walking very close, wriggling and dragging her feet but not shouting because he had a gun. They said that if anyone ever tries to abduct you from a crowded place, if they have a gun stabbing you through their coat, a knife in your back . . .' – I gesture with my own knife to make the point – ' . . . the thing to do is pretend to faint, to slump and become a dead weight, because that way they have to *drag you* wherever they want to take you, and it will attract more attention. So they say, anyway. If you start screaming they might panic and kill you, so you have to play dead, and hope someone even takes any notice.'

'Esther, okay, what are we talking about here?'

I suck on my teeth and squeeze my eyes up, shrug.

'In retrospect, Seymour was always mad as a goat,' she says. 'He was up at 5 a.m. every day, down at the children's playground in Heaton Park doing push-ups and pull-ups on the climbing frame. And all he ate for six months was tuna flakes and canned pineapple. He was on a mission, so he thought. But he was firing on all cylinders and hitting the target . . . not at all. I suppose because it happened so gradually . . . I thought nothing of it when he'd sit in his armchair all evening making a crucifix from a spatula and a wooden spoon, *fending off* anyone who called round.'

I've never heard of this person before. Conceivably Donna is making him up. I poke at my vegetables. I'm waiting for ten o'clock. I have an appointment to renew an old acquaintance of my own.

I take two buses to Hulme, where I wait in the middle of the Arch for a phone call with further instructions. When it comes I walk down to the Asda car park. There are no people about; a white mist hangs ghost-lit in the empty intersections. I sit on a wall behind the bike rack and wait, with my scarf pulled over my head and my hands jammed under my armpits. The cold mauve sky soars flat and featureless behind the mazes of homes around here.

The van appears around a corner eventually, parks up opposite me, and then they all stumble out of the back looking like a scuffle in a cartoon: a tangle of folding skinny dusty denim legs and arms. Except one of his friends is wearing a silver space helmet and two of the others have Stetsons and long silky capes on over their jean jackets. There are crude yellow felt moons and stars sewn on. None of them has seen me. Then James gets out of the passenger's side. This evening he's wearing a bright orange jumpsuit. He takes a pointy blue hat from the passenger seat and pulls it on, tugging the wide, bouncing brim right down. Then he leans back into the van, reaching in under his seat for a cardboard box full of spray cans, and then paint tins that he stacks up to make a pyramid on the pavement. James is short and stoop-shouldered, and he always looks like he's in a righteous temper. It's in the way he walks, moves, everything. Mostly it's in his eyes, but right now they're just under the wavy shadow his hat brim's casting. I suddenly think I can't stand it if I can't see his eyes looking at me properly right now. So I push myself off the wall and stand and rub the grit off my palms, then I put my fists on my hips and call over.

'Hippies,' I say. 'Hooligans.'

His friend Ray waves at me. James nudges his hat up with two fingers: a pistol he's pulled from where a belt would be. There he is, his dark eyes not showing if he's surprised; he smiles, looks down and then up again. He's pleased with himself when he says,

'We're not hooligans – we're cooligans.'

'James, that's debatable,' I say.

They come and do this sometimes: on the sides of vacant buildings, on corrugated garage doors where the taggers don't come, that's their thing, late at night and dressed up. I sit on the wall now watching them make up a shuddering sunset, swirling oceans, swirling skies. Ray in the space helmet is striping in zigzagged red tepees.

I've known James since I first came to Manchester. He's always irritated the hell out of me. Our conversations are generally thrust and parry argument flirtations – he'd never admit that but it's true – during which one of us will hold the other's gaze for a beat too long, and then we'll both shake our heads and tut.

'So aren't you going to ask me about all my adventures while I was away?' I say. Then I yawn into my sleeve.

He looks round just for one second, looks up and smiles, sort of smiles, and says, 'No.'

Then turns back to his painting and starts adding some dodgy looking horses capering about the blue hillside.

'Why are you such a dick?' I say.

'Why are you out here in the rain?' he says and shrugs with his back to me.

When he's finished we walk through town together, slosh through eddies of yellow and black leaves in All Saints Park. He's taken his overalls off, but kept his blue nylon pointy hat on, with his jeans and anorak. He looks completely ridiculous. We pass a door on the side of one of the warehouses behind Oxford Road, opposite the empty Haçienda. It's been crow-barred open. The two sides of the lock now curl out like steel petals. I say we should look inside. We do and it's raining in there too, somehow. James looks up into the dripping blackness.

'If you had anything about you, you wouldn't have needed to go away to sort yourself out,' he says. 'You could have done it here. Why go to New York. Go to Davyhulme.'

'No disrespect to Davyhulme,' I say, 'but, like you, I'm something of a culture vulture.'

He grins at that. He has feathered lines at the corners of his eyes.

I shake my head. 'If I had anything about me . . . that's a little offensive. I don't know James. Talking to you always makes me feel so *wrathful*.'

He slams the heel of his hand on the slick brick wall above my shoulder, tilts his head to one side.

'Good,' he says.

Good. He slides his other hand across his wet fringe and a line of dirty water runs down in front of his ear. His hat is bent. He smiles at me. He acts like he knows what he's talking about. It's hilarious. Still, I'd hate to ever see him looking unsure in a situation. I'm a coward that way. He looks sharp and serious again now.

'Donna has a name for you, James,' I say, ducking under his arm and out into the street. 'Fun and Games.'

4

Since I got back to Manchester I'd say my life
is a maze: a maze with no middle, but that's not
the whole point. I'm wandering mute along
corridors, around corners, and I'm not close to
panic yet. I sleep with the curtains open and
wake up when the sun comes up, earlier every
day. Then my legs switch along, taking me here
and there that I don't even choose: past the
Library and up Market Street; behind the
Cathedral and the Music School; in the Arndale
Centre, past the Buddhist Centre. I buy some
fruit off the Church Street market for my lunch,
go in the bar to see Mary or Donna, then maybe
walk around the new multiplex. I blend my
breathing with the sounds in there: with the
escalators, shallow and hissing and forced through
the nose; or else with the deep unremitting
whoosh of the a/c, pulling slow stomachfuls in
and counting them out again. I extended this
idea for two nights last week and stayed in a

tiny room in the Gardens Hotel on Piccadilly Approach. Maybe a stupid waste of money, when my money's running out, but it calms me down: you can't hear your footsteps on the thick lobby carpet and there's the sealed window silence in the rooms; maybe with the hum of the kitchen's ventilator outside, or the vacuum in the corridor. The tightly tucked in sheets, the laminated fire safety instructions, the smooth MDF furniture: you could be anywhere, nowhere. I imagined I could split those sheeny chintz curtains and see that: a calm blank, a glowing white nothingness.

When it's halfway warm I spend time in the gardens behind Victoria Station. I'm all for the dedicated public space. There it's all well-tended grass and artsy fountain arrangements; straight streams in grey granite troughs and stone benches with no backs. I lay down on one of them last Sunday and watched the people walking out of morning worship: a middle-aged woman with a blue blazer over her floral dress, a man with two children who gave him their shoes and went paddling. His wife stamped her feet and told them they'd get a cold. I pressed my thumbs on to my headphones for a second then just pulled them out and listened to the fountain noise.

I go to the pictures because it's warm in there

when it's cold outside. I like the early shows on weekdays because I'm usually the only person in, and so I can switch up the armrests and lay out. I put my Walkman on and if it's a bright, flashing film – and most of them are, let's face it – I read, or write in my detective notebook. Otherwise I can have a one-eye-shut sleep; keeping watch to snap up to attention if one of the goosy ticket checkers pokes their head in. While I was curled up in there today I noticed my jeans smelt of mildew, so when I got home I put them in the bath with some of Donna's vanilla shampoo and poked them with the mop handle; I had the lights out and listened to the Radar Brothers while I swirled them round and round.

What I'm thinking is that this routine I have is like saying alms; like lighting the candles and banging the beads; like lying on a rest-room floor saying the Jesus Prayer. Well, I'm sure I can feel something sometimes. This way may be trodden flat but if I keep going something is sure to click. I've stopped drinking so much too. Like I said to Donna, 'I'm off the slippery slope and on to the shining path.'

She's been out most evenings recently: rehearsing with her band in their room at the Beehive Mill after work and stopping out with her new fellow after that. Donna has lots of love affairs, but her heart belongs to her pen pal – remember them? – who's a fully quiffed up and intermittently syphilitic merchant seaman. His real name I don't know; she only ever calls him Billy Rocker. She's forever addressing postcards to foreign parts: Mauritius, Abu Dhabi, Copenhagen. His letters arrive at the bar. He writes on thick paper in tiny, neat, blockish capitals: splicing accounts of how he was 'wry and pithy' with his first mate in inappropriate circumstances with tales of more lugubrious misadventures and subsequent afternoons spent sweating on plastic chairs in heat-bound doctors' waiting rooms. He sent her a Polaroid of his desk in his cabin: a comb and a mirror, a pipe and a fountain pen, a picture of her. Donna's glasses hide her greatest asset, a fact not lost on Billy Rocker. He once wrote:

DONNA, THERE ARE LEG MEN AND THERE ARE BREAST MEN. DONNA, I AM AN EYEBROW MAN.

Donna's smitten. All she read for ages were books set at sea. It was the same with the films we watched, anything salt-flecked on the Central

Library shelves, she came home with: *The Last Detail, Billy Budd, L'Atalante, Jaws* . . . She had an ancient cast recording of *HMS Pinafore*; she played it in the bar, sang along with the tremulous, scratch-stuttered choruses. He sent her a button off his blazer: it had an anchor embossed on it. And she always wears a bracelet he made her by plaiting together copper wire and stiff rope flax while he was on whale watch. Well, Donna said he was on whale watch. Do they still have whale watch?

While she's been out – I'm going to have to use this word – gallivanting, recently I've been hanging out some evenings with Scottish Mary, an altogether different proposition. I try and wind Donna up talking about it. Last night she said:

'Mary this, Mary that. I've had enough. I'm leaving you.'

'Where would you go?' I said. I slammed my hand on the kitchen table. 'You're nothing without me.'

She planted her tiny chin on her tiny fist and closing one eye said, 'I'm going to move into the *Evening News* stationery cupboard – like Maeve Brennan at *The New Yorker*. I've been thinking about it for a while.'

I nodded. 'You could sleep in a big padded envelope,' I said.

'And shoot people with staples when they come in.' She mimed quick-drawing two staple guns at me.

'It sounds fantastic,' I said. 'I'm all about stationery. I'll go and pack. And I'm having the top shelf, by the way.'

'Okay,' she said, then shook her tatty hair. 'What? *What*? Wait a moment . . .'

Mary comes from Edinburgh. She's in the third year of a photography degree at the Met. When I was round at her flat in Fallowfield last week she told me about her most recent project. I suppose it could be seen as morally dubious. I wouldn't argue with that. I'd probably just shrug. She put a sweet and submissive personal ad in *City Life* magazine and soon found herself in possession of several voicemail messages. She still has them on her Dictaphone. She played them for me, the 'anyway's, the 'hope to hear's, the coughs and the pauses, and I watched her eyes harden and her smile spread. She went on elaborate dates with these men: dinner, dancing, then desertion: she took a one-way trip to the Ladies. All the while her friend hid and took pictures.

'Behind the potted plants with a zoom lens,' I said.

'Exactly,' she said, and pressed her lips together and made big eyes, sliding the slippy plastic pages of her portfolio folder over on the kitchen table. 'I like this one where I've gone to the bar. Look, he's doing his hair.'

She laughed and laughed. They're good photos, without doubt. You can't look at them and not feel something.

What I like about Mary is the walk, the hip sway. I've been studying it. If a person walks like she walks they can go anywhere and they won't feel like they're on their hands and knees like I sometimes do. I know I shouldn't but I do.

She's leaving for Paris in a couple of months. She wants to get a job as a chamber maid in a hotel there and then take pictures of people's things in their rooms while they're out.

'Get some kind of narrative going on,' she said.

I should offer up a little more relevant history, some snapshots from my past. My first boyfriend, Richard, was twenty-five when we met. I was seventeen. On our first date he told me he tended to fancy young girls who dressed too old, or middle-aged women who dressed too young. I was having a 1940s phase, so I certainly qualified. Daytimes I was in tea dresses and librarian shoes; evenings was flouncy flowery slips with baseball boots. These always with a tweedy coat and my hair held up same as now, with a Biro.

He used to call me his little doll. He used to say, Look at your little big eyes. Your face is so pretty. Your mouth is so pretty. That's why it's pleasurable for me to watch when you . . .

I was too young to work at the bar with Donna, so I was passing the days in the café across the road from her. Richard used to come in and buy espressos and stare over his news-paper.

One day he said, 'So are you going to come for a drink with me or what?'

I was so surprised I said 'What?' and he thought I was being funny.

I thought he was nice-looking: tall with duck-lingy blond hair and blotchy fair skin. He kind of dressed like he was from the forties too. Another thing he said on our first date was, 'The girl of my dreams doesn't hold her glass like that.'

Once, when we'd been going out for a few months, we were watching a film at his place and I wrote I LOVE YOU with my finger on his back, through his checked shirt. He didn't acknowledge it until the film was finished and the tape was rewinding, whirring and clicking.

He said, 'You do know I'm still seeing other people?'

'No,' I said.

He turned round then and said, 'Is your heart hurt?'

He always squinted to show sincerity. Is your heart hurt. I said he behaved like he hated me.

He said, 'I wouldn't have slept with you if I hated you. Not repeatedly, anyway.'

Every now and then these other girlfriends of his came to see him when he was working. He was a DJ three nights a week at a bar in Chorlton. They didn't say anything when they saw me, sitting behind him on the stack of record boxes. They just smiled. He drank a bottle of whisky a night in there. He said it made him feel serene.

Once when we got back to his house afterwards he climbed up on his crumbling front wall with a bottle in his hand. His flagpole-thin body bent forwards then backwards while he got his balance. Then he put his fists in the air and closed his eyes and shouted: 'Every woman in the world wants to suck my cock.'

In my bedsit the next morning I got into one of my states: sitting in a corner of the sofa bed and crying and crying: everything was slow dissolving and I was smearing at the pooling of mascara and tears then wiping my fingers on the wall, until my eyelashes were sleek and soft and clean like they hadn't been for months and there was an ashy finger painting over the dado rail.

In the window of the Empire Exchange shop on Oxford Road, propped up between rusting tin toys and vintage porn, was a framed Penny Black stamp. Richard told me he'd always wanted to steal it. He thought it was a very *Boy's Own* escapade: once he'd taken it he wanted to 'scarper'. He had it well planned out: go into town late, do press-ups in the car park opposite the BBC to keep himself warm until there was no one about. He'd wear something no one could say was his, like a tracksuit, and pull his woolly hat right down. He'd take a brick for the window from his front wall. And as soon as the burglar alarm started he'd run behind India House and get a taxi. He talked about it late at night when we lay and listened to the rain. Another thing he talked about was something he'd heard on Radio 4: about these caves under the ice in Antarctica, where plants and flowers still grew. He used to bring it up a lot. We'd pretend we were there and all that.

Some of the things he told me you'd think a person would keep private. He told me about a night when he and his sixth-form sweetheart, Natalie, went to see Throwing Muses and he got so angry that she was paying more attention to the music than to him that he wanted to punch her in the face. While he was telling me this I looked at the picture of her in his photomontage of exes over his desk. She was the prettiest, standing under a tree looking stern, hair in a henna'd bob, wearing a big V-neck jumper, a flowery skirt and DMs. When they split, he told me, she told some of their friends that he'd beaten her up. It was late one night he was telling me about that. We were in bed. He looked into the distance and said:

'I was fucking angry at her at the time, but now I think I was drunk a lot then, and . . .' here he squinted and lifted his chin up to a suitably noble angle – he was revealing his innermost after all – 'maybe I did.' He squinted and shook his head slowly, *in wonder*: said again, '*Maybe I did.*'

I didn't reply. I couldn't be bothered. I wouldn't

67

be surprised at anything he'd done. He'd shout at me for anything, and jab his finger in my shoulder when he did. Once when he did that I wet myself. He said I'd done it deliberately to have a go at him. Maybe I did. Who knows? You're just like Natalie, he said. One time he gaffer-taped me bent over his kitchen chair, a few times to the bed, then he'd stuff my knickers in my mouth and hit me with his fancy vintage forties belt. Why didn't I leave? Well, no one had ever looked at me before. I know it's pathetic. Still, I think when I was crying during those incidents I was really crying over other things about myself. I was lost back then. When I did finally finish with him I wanted him to say sorry for the way he'd been to me and what he'd done. I even thought I would stay with him if he did.

He said, 'My only regret is that I never fucked you hard enough.'

When I was away for a while after that he didn't come to see me. No one did except Donna. A package arrived there though, and it was that Penny Black, in its splintering plywood frame. He wrote a song about me, too, called 'Little Doll'. Did he expect me to be flattered by that? For his sake I hope not.

What makes me go cold now is that some women end up pulling their own guts out for men like that their whole lives. But not me. I had that thought while I was out walking yesterday. When I used to think about that time I felt I was wading through a swamp: horror show creepers helter-skeltering up my legs; all fibrous and slimy, twining around my throat; pushing into my mouth and everywhere else they felt like. But I smiled and closed my eyes battling the wind coursing down Market Street yesterday. Smiled and felt my dry lips crack at the corners as I paddled along the sopping wet pavement. Not me. I appreciate that I reserve an apostate's rage and scorn for Richard. I'm most angry at myself. Then again, you have to learn about the world sometime and I learnt early and that's good. In the spirit of his considered *aperçu* on our relationship I'll say that my only regret is that my body didn't reject his demon seed on principle. Save me a job.

I moved in with Donna soon after that. She came and got me, carried my three cardboard boxes of books and CDs and clothes downstairs while I waited in the car. I went back to just reading and writing for a few months. Then with the next boy I was seeing I didn't know what to do, so I clicked myself into this terrible fake frenzy of porno speak and flip-flopping about. He bought it, he liked that, which certainly made me think. Then with the next one, the last one, a sweet and simple soul who I liked a lot, I was nothing, just a dead body. That may be how he put it too. But that's old news. Soon after that I stopped altogether. If boys stayed over they kept their jeans on. I curled up away from them pretending to be too drunk and sleepy. Anything else only gave me that old feeling of hysterical loneliness. I don't know what to do about that. I was always inclined to think, Why should I do anything about it? But that's just defeatist.

Sometimes I pick up Donna's guitar, but all I've ever learnt to play is this fiddly finger-picked tune, this looping accusatory melody. I sometimes sit in the kitchen chair playing it over and over, nodding along with my eyes closed, and I'm sure my pocket-sized pal would have something to say about the significance of that.

5

It's the last day of March and I'm standing at the dripping, steam-filmed kitchen window. Donna sits behind me at the table with a tea and a book. I can hear her turning pages. I can hear her breathing over my own.

'What are you up to tomorrow?' She says eventually, 'It's my day off.'

'It's your off day?' I say, looking round.

She lifts one hand and then slices it down, miming a slow return shot. She says, 'We are terrific ping pong players.'

I suck my invisible cigarette. There aren't any clouds this evening. Above the traffic everything is awesomely still, the sky is cold and clear.

'Well, ringing the changes, I'm having a day out in the city,' I say, and turn my chair backwards before I sit down. 'Swinging on lampposts, trying on hats, hair at two, nails at three . . .'

'Sounds good,' she says. I lean back to watch

the moths twirling upwards around the bare bulb in here.

'You think?' I say. 'You coming with then?'

I tap my invisible cigarette into her mug then stand up again. I do feel restless.

'Barring better offers,' she says.

I look back out of the window and press my forehead and the inside of both my wrists against the icy glass.

I'm up early as usual the next day. I put a tape on in the kitchen while I make a pot of tea, then I take Donna's cup in to her. I've put on the clothes I was wearing this time last year: no less of a sodden approximation of the season than this, still I took it upon myself to wear a pair of old red ballet shoes around town. In the mornings I would put one foot at a time up on my chilly windowsill to crisscross the frayed ribbons up my calves. They were always coming undone and trailing behind me. By the time I got home from work at the bar each night the ends were blackened, beer-soaked. But I've got them on today with my green Willa Cather prairie dress and my cardigan.

I look up and watch Donna get dressed. She's only tiny. When she folds her leg up to pull on her jeans her plumped-up thigh is swagged with oyster-coloured stretch marks, like cat stripes, like the rents in dull clouds where the winter sun shows through.

'There's this white crinoline skirt in Oxfam,' she says. 'I've going to buy it to go with my anorak, sort of the look of an H.G. Wells space Victorian,' she says, mashing a tiny hand about in her sticking-out hair, 'for this gig in Leeds tomorrow, which you're coming to, by the way.'

I nod. Donna's had a couple of Victorian phases. When she first got her car she drove us out to the Brontë parsonage. She wrote in the visitors' book comments section:

They're here! They're here! Hello?

I liked it there. Through Emily's window the huge flat slab gravestones looked like the pages of a book laid out in disarray. My favourite Brontë is Bramwell. No, that's not true. That's me being flippant.

I think I need to cough. There's something tickling in my neck. In fact there's something strange coming up. I lift my mug to catch it. I can hear sticky noises in my stomach. It doesn't hurt. It pours out slowly: a golf ball-sized cluster of soft white foam, tipping over my bottom lip. Then another and another one. Tiny stiff bubbles.

I raise my eyes and look at Donna. She's looking like she might laugh.

'It's finally happened,' she says. 'Perhaps you should actually eat something today.'

I get up and go over to her mirror to stare down my throat and see what gives. While I'm there I put my make-up on: inky mascara and pale lipstick.

I put on Donna's black anorak and fix my hair up in a low ponytail, with a greying fabric flower as well as the Biro. I'm looking forward to today.

As we wait for the bus I lift one foot then the other and rub my toes along my shins. The puddle dirt dries quickly in pale powdery stripes. Donna's rolled her jeans up, she's got my red-ribbed socks on. They look good.

For breakfast she buys us an avocado each from her friend Clive's stall by the university. We sit down in the garden outside Central Library and eat them with our fingers. It's such a damp day, we're the only people lingering there. Two Italian boys come and mutter near us for ages before asking me to take their picture in front of a red telephone box. I have to wipe the green slime off my hands on my cardigan first.

We walk through Albert Square and down to Waterstone's, where we wander around the ground floor for a while, picking books up and then putting them down again. Donna has a crush on the boy at the biography desk so we have to go upstairs and walk past him a couple of times.

'Don't look,' she says. 'We'll stand by that display table and I'll just ache in his direction.'

We do that. Then Donna tells me:

'I was in here before work the other day. I was half-conscious in *Lit Crit*, dog-tired, and I was leaning with my forehead on one of the shelves,' she demonstrates this, and keeps talking, but quietly, 'I found myself listening in to the conversation at the counter. It was this young French student cliché: Benetton top, backpack, plimsolls, he was saying: Eh, excuse me, do you know the Shakespeare? Do you have a book explaining the Shakespeare? I was listening in and I got the giggles a bit over his accent.' Here she starts laughing madly at herself. 'Then I noticed that I'd been drooling down my top. There were these two strings of spit hanging there to my knees nearly.'

I roll my eyes.

'Donna,' I say, 'sometimes your lack of formal education really shows.'

'I know it,' she says.

I tell Donna all about this bloke I went out with a couple of times while I was away, because he said things like:

'Those Columbia critical theory professors: they are some bad-ass motherfuckers. I'm telling you, they could dissect a *newt*.'

One night he took me to a frat house Halloween party, of all things, in a cavernous Upper West Side apartment. He said we should at least look at the roof garden, although it was too cold to stay out very long. Maybe he wanted us to be alone, but there was someone else up there already, standing with his back to us, looking out at the mist-swathed city. As we walked across to him my date told me in hushed tones that his father owned something. I forget what. I didn't have a costume, but my date had said, 'You'll do.'

He was dressed as Humphrey Bogart: shirt sleeves and suspenders with his hair slicked back and a thin cigarette dangling. This other fellow was wearing a sailor suit with a painted cardboard porthole stuck on his big proud belly and a plastic seagull perched on one of his broad shoulders. Smashed polystyrene boulders were held in the squeaking Cellophane which was twisted round his ankles. My date introduced us and then they talked for a while. I leant over the stone balustrade and smoked an invisible cigarette.

As we left to go back downstairs sailor boy called to me, 'Hey, I have something for you.'

His cheeks were little red cherries. His smile was sloppy. He stuffed his hand in the pocket of his tight white trousers to prise out a sheaf of paper tickets. He handed one to me. Printed on it, professionally printed on it:

FREE RIDE ON THE TITANIC

Big laughs all round. I laughed too and patted his free shoulder.

We spend the dim afternoon hours in the art gallery on Mosley Street, sitting cross-legged on benches drawing pictures in the pads we bought from the gift shop. We neither of us know one end of a pencil from the other, but still.

We go and buy Donna's space Victorian skirt, then we walk to the end of a crowded Deansgate, dodging through slow moving families and couples. We take the lift to the top of the multi-storey car park behind the AMC cinema, and then start to walk slowly down the steep concrete ramp that Scalextric curves around outside it. The sky has been thickening all day, and we stop and look up at the low clouds, ruptured here and there with garish neon white. Always when the weather's like this, spoiling for a storm, I have to be outside and see the sky amber, dark and light at the same time, flashing, then finally, in a beat, the raindrops shattering everywhere. It doesn't happen quite yet and so an obscure restlessness keeps working inside me as Donna and I edge down the slope together against an unsure wind, both of us listening for cars.

We decide to go home for tea before we hit the town. In the supermarket on our way back, Donna starts getting the fear. I look up from the vegetables and see her turning a corner up ahead, holding her small arms out stiff and doing a creaky, swaying robot walk. The basket in her hand is swinging into a tower of biscuit boxes. I catch up with her. She twists her head around slowly and she's got her dead eyes in. When she drops her basket I hear the frozen meals crack. I pay for some veg and then go outside and find her sitting on the fire exit steps behind the trolley train. She's got her glasses off. She looks like Balthus's *Thérèse Dreaming*. She still does. She always will. She smiles when she sees me.

'Sorry,' she says, rubbing her gems on her coat, 'I had to get out of there.'

She seems weary, so I give her the dubious benefit of my peculiarly good mood. I hose her with happiness and optimism. As we walk through the cold I'm swinging my shoulders in my anorak and saying:

'I think many exciting things happen if you're open to life, Donna. You just have to act like you are and then events come your way. I sincerely believe that. If you send out the right signals.'

She couldn't agree more.

'That's why those shag-tag club nights are such a great thing,' she says.

Very droll.

The storm finally starts just after the sun goes down. Heavy rain plashes all around us as we're walking past the Science and Industry Museum. We go to a pub near the flat where Donna lived with her gran, a place we used to frequent after our walks when we were teenagers, both of us in our black cords, tin badges on our cardigans. We would commandeer a corner and whisper private jokes. The jukebox had old punk tunes on it then and the students from the college across the way would stand round the pool table, drinking long Cokes and watching *Rising Damp* on the silent portable.

I always used to underline things in my books about days like that. Marina Tsvetaeva:

Clattering with gold pieces, and
slowly puffing out smoke, we
walk like solemn foreigners
throughout my native city.

and Adrienne Rich. Something about *our hair blazing* . . . something something . . . *our bodies young and ordinary* . . . My hair blazes; Donna's, blown like it is now, into a wispy smudge, is like smoke.

I also think of the *South Bank Show* Smiths documentary we watched together years and years ago: Linder Sterling saying that her and Morrissey went on long walks together: 'very intimate but very separate at the same time'. That's my credo for friendship. I've had many insights into life so far today, pulling my Biro out regularly to write them in my detective notebook, or inside my arm if we were on the move.

Today in the pub we notice curling carnations and drooping ferns on the lapels of the people coming out of the back room. The men's faces are red and rumpled, the women's hats askew. Donna grins up at one of them:

'Have you had a smashing wedding?' she says.

The woman just nods and clip-clops past quickly. We're both a little hazy at this point I think. We drink a lot faster than we did. We try to gatecrash the reception, but Donna's got her soggy All Stars on so they won't let us.

Out in the cold again, she says, 'I've let the side down,' and looks at her shoes, sadly.

'No,' I say, 'you've kept the end up.'

The rain is still twitching on the pavements and on the beer garden tabletops. We lie down along the wet benches and look up at the buildings: mostly ghostly, lit-up offices, one low-rise residential block.

'I'm never going to be as tall as those,' Donna says. I can't disagree.

I tell her about someone else I met when I was away, one night when I went for a walk uptown and wound up sitting down in a park facing the East River. The weather was just turning cold, but the old man on the other end of my seat wasn't dressed for it: he was head to toe in white sports gear: trainers, knee socks, shorts and a polo shirt. His stout legs were tanned, hairless. He rested his ankle on his knee and his glossy calf fell in a slack swag. His face was ancient and his eyes were milky. He had some good material: stories of riding home sitting on the hoods of gypsy cabs, of waking up under his uncle's baby grand. I could picture him young and jaunty in flannels and wing-tip shoes. I'm a sucker for a park-bench raconteur. He called me 'miss' and himself 'the General' and when he found I was new in town he pointed out some of the things twinkling along the skyline: the Triboro Bridge, the Hell's Gate Bridge, Roosevelt Island, Ward Island, Shea Stadium.

'And up there's heaven,' he said and twitched his head skywards. The girl at the next bench looked up.

Donna says, 'Long distance runners always look to God in the final stretch.'

We try that on our way to the Star and Garter for lasties. But we both get dizzy and go off course.

Inside, there are kids emptying out after a gig upstairs, two lanky girls are playing snooker and there's a man sitting at the bar who I know, I'm sure. He's got one hand mashed in his thick brown hair and he's writing on scraps of paper sideways. He keeps looking up at me while I'm taking my coat and cardigan off and then, while I'm kneeling to retie my shoe ribbons, I look up and he's watching me.

Donna and I sit down across the room with our double gins. I keep irritating Donna by looking over her shoulder while she's talking. I know that I know this fellow, so I'm just staring across the snooker table and making my eyes ask him how.

Donna huffs and lets her head fall back. She says she wants to leave because she has to be up early, and I'm not being great company all told. We're both just swinging our legs and drinking too fast. I don't mind that so much, but, okay, we leave, and we get as far as Piccadilly, where the cab line curves into the station. The cars' tyres send up a ghostly white spray as they process past us. Donna's counting her money to see if we can afford one when I make a decision. I give her a note from my wallet, and then start walking backwards with my hands in my coat pockets and stray curls of hair blowing in my face.

'Yeah,' I say, 'I'm going to go back and get that bloke.'

'What bloke?'

'He was sitting at the bar. We were making eyes at each other, I think.'

'And you're going to go and get him?' She just looks bemused.

'Yeah,' I nod, 'I think so. Yes.'

'Well, okay,' she says. 'I'm going to go and stay at whatsisname's then.' She shakes her soaked and heavy legs one by one and says, 'The rain's pulling my trousers down anyway. Ten o'clock tomorrow though remember. I would say have fun . . .'

I push my sleeves up and crack my knuckles and grin. She raises her phenomenal eyebrows, then I turn around to walk back up Fairfield Street. I don't feel odd. No idea of embarrassment. I run back up to that bar actually.

And he's sitting on the doorstep, waiting for me. I think I knew he would be. He must have watched me leave and come back. Imagine that. He smiles and lifts one hand up, says Hey there.

Newton — that's his name — isn't dressed very seriously: his shoes are green, his coat has checks all over it. As he walks along his jeans go *swick-swick-swick* because the rain water has soaked up nearly to his knees. He's from Vermont, turns out, and his band played support upstairs tonight. But his friends have all left him, to sleep in their clothes on the promoter's living-room floor.

'And I thought I'd just hang out there by the door and see if that cute girl came back . . .'

That would be me then. When he said that he squeezed one side of his face up and smiled. A fantastic smile, really. His mouth all dark and scored looking. He's a drinker, I could tell, by how the plum colour of his lips blended out. So I asked if he might want to come and get a late one with me and he stood up and said, Let's go.

Now we're walking along Piccadilly Approach towards Oldham Street. He's twenty-nine, he tells me, but he looks probably ten years older than that, mainly on account of his scraggy beard and his big round stomach. His tatty brown hair is growing out over the collar of his overcoat and in a curling-up fringe. He asks if I'm a student and I say no, and then I have to tell him what I am. So then we have to talk about books. How I hate doing that with strangers, but his first question is: Have you read Denis Johnson? I look at him sideways when he asks that. Yeah, I say, and I get carried away and quote *Already Dead*, the description of Melissa:

'Let me tell you about this girl. Her eyes are brown and wet . . . Eyes that are never going to look at anyone again . . . A woman this vulnerable and perverse . . .'

I think I hit him with pretty much the whole page.

'Yeah, that's a good passage,' he says, and he smiles and nods and looks at me sideways. He's a scruff: his whole demeanour makes me think of pinching a pigeon feather and brushing it backwards.

I point down Portland Street to the bulb-bobbled Britannia Hotel, and at the grubby portico of the Gardens Hotel, as we pass, hung tonight with a rain-stained vinyl sign advertising cheap rooms. I tell him they're where I go when I pretend I'm getting away.

'I do things like that where I'm from,' he says and nods.

We walk up Oldham Street. I'm having a fine time talking to someone new. I show him a couple of examples of Manc monkey walkers up ahead and then we stop to pet the enormous wet duvet of a dog that guards the late shop. A hefty orange and black animal, it's slumped under the bus shelter chewing its paw. I've never found out its name. Outside the bar, the street's tiny contingent of teenage Mods are standing in a rigid group: lean boys in shiny suits and girls in shift dresses and white tights, stamping and shivering, frowning while they tweak their hairdos in the window.

'Timecops,' I whisper to Newton, with one hand cupped around my mouth. 'The reason they look like they're from 1965 is that they are from 1965.'

He nods. 'You have to stop looking guilty then,' he says.

I take his hand so the bouncer knows he's with me, and we go inside. It's rammed busy. Mary's working with another girl who I don't recognise: a short Chinese girl with her pinkish tinted hair in a messy topknot, wearing a shirt dress and football socks under her go-go boots, the red striped tops folded down. Mary gives me a quick wave and nods to Newton. The advantage of height, she can see everything going on in here. When he's not looking she raises an eyebrow at me. I take his coat to put behind the bar with mine then I get some generous drinks. I pass Newton his whisky and tell him to come downstairs, the only place where it will be quiet enough to talk.

We lean our shoulders against the streaky tiles by the stockroom. People keep walking past who I haven't seen since I got back. I try not to catch their eye.

Newton says, 'Do you have a lot of boyfriends in here tonight?'

'No,' I say. 'No. Recently, I've been living from the neck up.'

Here I draw one hand slowly across my throat.

He tilts his head on one side and squeezes one eye up.

He says, 'Listen,' and looks at me some more. 'Do you feel like falling in love this evening?' Then, 'You know I watched you walk in to the bar tonight with your friend. You took your jacket off and your cardigan off. Then your bra strap fell below your dress . . .'

He touches the top of my arm and smiles some. He looks in my eyes and I kind of squint over his shoulder then look back at him.

'I'm never normally affectionate with people I've just met, but everything you're saying . . . it's very weird,' he says.

Then he says I should give him a hug, so okay. I keep my eyes open. His greasy hair feels cold in my hand. My other hand is on his shirt which is sweat-stuck to his back. My chin is on his shoulder. I step back and look away, look around.

'You seem kind of uncomfortable,' he says. 'What's over there? Is there a reflective surface?' He widens his sleepy eyes at me.

'Yeah,' I say. I look at the blotchy mirror advertising beer, then back at him.

'It's not vanity. It's insecurity. I have low self-esteem.' I nod at him and smile. 'I can trace it all back to an incident in my childhood.'

He nods and takes my hands in his.

'Me too,' he says. 'I can trace it all back to an incident: my childhood.' He twitches an eyebrow.

'Let's go back upstairs,' I say.

The bar is still full with the student crowd all drunk and messy, dancing, leaning against the walls. We sit down on the edge of the stage together. Behind us a band are setting up. We swig our drinks. I swing my legs and look around. The boys are rickets thin, the girls have doughy stomachs squishing over the tops of their jeans. They lurch around us in tight embraces.

'I've noticed how kids here really like to make out with each other in public,' Newton says. He has his head tilted on one side, his hair throwing ragged shadows over his eyes. 'That really doesn't happen where I'm from. It's kind of nasty, don't you think?'

'Yes it is,' I say, 'kind of nasty.'

There's a whole row of blue moons hanging behind him now. Their glow smears on his face. I push his hair back to see his eyes. His smile makes kitten whisker creases across his temples. Then I kiss him.

'I'm sorry,' I say. I press my lips together. 'Now we're both vulgar exhibitionists.'

'Not at all, I think you should be bold more often,' he says.

'You think,' I say and nod to myself and smile to myself.

'I'm still falling in love,' he says.

'I thought we might have dissipated the tension with that kiss,' I say. He shakes his head. He puts a finger in the ripped seam of my cardigan, runs it along the rent.

'You're coming apart,' he says.

'Oh, I know it,' I say. Then, 'Shall we get out of here?'

Newton stands up and looks at me. He sticks out his stomach and pats it. He says, 'Yeah. Let's shoot the route, kid.'

I ask Mary to call us a cab. We sit on the ledge out front waiting. I can see everywhere on Oldham Street I've worked over the last few years. As I point them out to Newton I see myself in those places again: smiling at customers who bought something I liked in Vinyl Exchange; folding musty seconds in Oxfam Originals; elbows on the counter in the Northern Quarter Café. Newton tells me he works as a waiter sometimes himself. I look at him and try to imagine that. Above the shops opposite some people are standing out on their shallow balconies: one bleary-eyed girl in pyjamas and a woolly hat leans over the metal grill to drop keys to her boyfriend.

As cars swish past and the cold sky clears, as we're talking, I keep on thinking, words like *redemptive*, words like *transformative*, they float through my mind: all that odd ennobling vocabulary, all cut loose. Inside, behind us, a band keep starting and stopping the same number. Again and again there's the brittle noise of the sticks counting time then they crash in together all wrong.

We're kissing as soon as we get into the flat: sliding to sit with our backs to the front door first off, his legs drawn up in front of him and me, I just can't keep still. I have to keep shaking myself out of just looking at him. Putting one hand on his bristly beard and just staring. Then smiling. Then staring. He smiles back. He strokes my hair, he says my name, he asks me questions.

I stand up and pull him up too, then his back bashes the doorframe as I steer him into my bedroom, manoeuvre him in past the boxes with a drunks-do-the-last-dance walk. I hit the light in the hallway: off, the small light in my room: on.

'Airlock effect,' I say and shut the door behind us.

I sit down. He stands in front of the door with his hands by his sides. I look in his eyes and I can see – he's in a strange cold bedroom in a strange cold town. We're here together, though, that's something.

My room is a barren tip. The boxes are still stacked in the corners, the bare duvet is on the floor by the record player and there are half-full mugs and scraps of scrawled-on paper everywhere.

'As you can see: I'm currently – riding the crest of a slump,' I say. 'Excuse the . . .'

I sweep a hand around the carnage, but he isn't looking anywhere except at me. There are unfinished books everywhere: resting open on my bed like pitched roofs, like dead birds. He picks one up as he sits down next to me.

'These are what you put your arms around at night,' he says.

'Yeah,' I nod at my knees then look right at him. 'They're not very responsive.'

Later on I'm raking the herringbone pattern of hair on his sticking out stomach and he looks at my arm: the writing on the inside and the silvery slice scars on the outside.

He says, 'Now baby I know you don't have a cat you've been brawling with.'

I feel so calm, such relief, I don't say a word. He has sleepy eyes and a squashed nose, a patchy beard. My eyes can't stop moving over his face, the thread veins' fuchsia cross-stitch on his pallid skin, all the pores on his nose plugged with dirt. He's just great looking all told. I feel like he's an angel, that's what I want to call him.

'What's the matter?' he says and I just smile and look at him more. Nothing the matter. I like his voice. I like watching his mouth work while he's talking.

He says, 'Is it that . . . you want to make love to me?'

He raises his eyebrows.

I say, 'The thing about me is – I'm really quite shy.'

I look in his eyes.

'You shouldn't be nervous,' he says. 'I'm the one looking at a beautiful naked girl.'

'I'm not naked,' I say, 'I mean, I'm not nervous.'

He lies down next to me.

He says, 'You know – you have a face to die for.'

'Well, don't die,' I say, 'we just met.'

In the morning I have to leave at eight to catch the train to Leeds to meet Donna. Drinking my tea, waiting for my cab to come, I stand in the bedroom doorway: there he is in my bed, facing the wall, his knees drawn up, his arms outside the duvet. I feel calm and nervous both. I leave him a note with the name of a bar in Liverpool where we can meet after his gig there tonight. I stand in the cold, green and yellow-tiled stair-well for must be a minute, holding the flat door open, turning on the spot in that dank and echoic space, feeling that I'm not me and the sunless day out there is somewhere else, too. The cabby's leaning on his horn now but I go back in the flat again quickly to give Newton another kiss goodbye. I hold his tatty head in my hands and do that.

7

Looking up from my book when the train stops at Stockport, I see a boy get on the crowded carriage who I recognise as the younger brother of my ex-boyfriend, Lee. I can't remember his name. We only met once, at a messy party at their parents' house in Heaton Moor. That was nearly three years ago, his sixteenth. He looked like Lee back then; now it's much more marked, now that he's not so hopelessly gawky.

He stands by the luggage rack. He's absorbed in whatever's on his headphones. My Walkman is chugging in my pocket, but I turn it off now. How strange that I can watch him without self-consciousness. I don't need to feel furtive, sullen. I see him catch his reflection in the blackened glass in the door as we slip into a tunnel speeding up. He smoothes his curling black hair in front of his ears, but looks down and away quickly as though he doesn't like what he sees. Then he reads the map on the wall, looks at his shoes.

His jeans and jumper are just ordinary, not like all the daft fancy threads Lee started wearing before he moved away down South for good. But he stands the same way as his brother, with his shoulders pinched up. His expression is blank: elsewhere. I read my book again for a while, but I start thinking I want to see this kid smile Lee's smile. I'd like it for him to see me and smile, in fact.

A lot of people shuffle off at Sheffield, and he sinks into a seat diagonally opposite me: his elbows on the table with my paper and my two empty cardboard tea cups. He has his chin in one hand, he's staring nowhere. I get a funny feeling. Lee's eyes, those same eyes, used to look at me in a way that they won't anymore, and here it is literally realised, because neither would this kid remember or know. Looking at him feels like getting no answer when you phone and you know someone's in. All those familiar mannerisms – smoothing his hair and looking away from the mirror. I put it out of my mind when I get off the train.

I find Donna supervising while the boys in her band unload the equipment at Joseph's Well. We leave them to it and go to get drunk and walk around, like we always do when she has a show. She asks me about my night. I tell her,

'I can't talk about it yet, suffice to say, there was a little bit of romance in the air. Yes there was.'

She's okay with that, she's busy psyching herself up, her eyebrows are drawn together in a deep, dark V. She gets nervous, though she wouldn't admit that.

Tonight her band play support. Usually she keeps her back to the audience, if there is one; tonight she stands almost side on. This may be progress, who knows? Still, she turns her pretty, pointed face away, stares at her effects pedals exclusively. I stay at the front, to one side. I have one hand spread flat on the nylon grill of the speaker. When they finish I wave to tell her I'm off. She nods and smiles through the smoke. I walk down to the station.

I'm in Liverpool by ten, and I go straight across to Ma Egerton's, opposite Lime Street. This is another pub Donna and I used to frequent when I was skiving and she came visiting. It's our kind of a place, small and smoky. Above the sturdy dado rail are framed old lobby cards from the Empire Theatre across the way: for the pantomimes, for Billy Fury and Cilla Black and Barnum's Circus. Donna and I would sit in here just sipping our drinks, underlining things in our Shelleys and Anne Sextons.

I get a double gin and go and wait in the snug. I keep smiling to myself and trying to hide it and then just grinning even more. My throat keeps tightening with happiness and then I have to laugh out loud and look at my hands and wonder what's going on. An old Scouse soak from the next table comes and sits next to me. He puts his slopping orange pint down and leans back.

'Look at you,' he says, 'you're loving life.'

He beams at me. He's all teeth and eyes: a bony creature with just a swirl of colourless hair, and angry skin on his nose and cheeks.

'Damn right,' I tell him.

We introduce ourselves. He's Jed.

'Your name is too long,' he says. 'I have a new name for you. Muggsy.'

That line probably works better for some people than others. So I frown and then smile.

'Muggsy? Okay.'

We shoot the breeze for a while. We're leaning back and looking at the old posters.

'These days,' he says, 'leisure is just colour being thrown at you. The first time I went to the cinema I was agog,' here he stares up, lets his nearly toothless mouth fall slack, 'looking at these huge figures – "Look at *that*! He's bigger than my *dad*!" We took our cap guns in with us for the cowboy flicks. Champion the Wonder Horse. He was supposed to be in the Empire panto one year,' he nods towards the theatre opposite, 'and my mum took me and my brothers, and halfway through, Here comes Champion! And this *donkey* skids across the stage, obviously just been pushed on, like . . .'

The etched, yellow glass door opens and there's Newton. He holds a hand up, says Hey.

'I'll check you later Jed,' I say and stand up.

'Okay, queen,' he says.

We sit in a corner and talk. It's an enjoyably frustrating conversation because our eyes keep meeting and we're both bringing up books and films that the other one hasn't heard of. He's never seen *Billy Liar*, for instance. I tell him my favourite line from that film: 'I turn over a new leaf every day, but the blots show through.'

'Do you ever get that feeling?' I ask him and he says he does. He does.

'This is what I call a cultural divide,' he says, shaking his head. 'We're going to have to meet on a street corner and swap suitcases sometime.

But, hey, I went and saw your book today. I was fixing my hair in the window of the shop, checking my breath before I looked on the shelf.'

He mimes all this, flatting his curly fringe down and then licking his thumb and forefinger to smooth his eyebrows. He hasn't bought one, he assures me, because yesterday I made him promise not to, just like I won't buy his records. I don't know why this seems of crucial importance to me.

'So I never get to read any of your stories?' he says now.

'You're asking me to share my maiden diaries . . . well, maybe, you know . . . *When you are old* . . .'

He rolls his eyes at that one. He says he can't imagine what my writing would be like and I say:

'Let's just say I'm of the expressive school.'

He nods sadly and says, 'Oh, me too.'

We both sigh dramatically and look at our knees.

Newton says a lot of thought-provoking things and I tell him so. Likewise, he says. We're new acquaintances, getting along, so conversation naturally turns to our deformities. I show him my inside out elbow. He lifts his thin shirt and T-shirt a little to show a puckered appendix scar, a cushioned sliver of crushed purple satiny skin. I didn't notice that before. Then he shows how his little fingers can bend outwards at the second knuckle. We put our palms together to look at the difference. Both of us wordsmiths, that's what we do.

He tells me about where he grew up. Then he says:

'I was an only child. My parents were both smart, but they were flighty, and they loved each other so much, more than they ever loved me. I had to do a lot for myself, from a young age. It wasn't great. Now I feel like my childhood is with me every day. Being alone. Being shut out. Some people, maybe they had a terrible time, maybe a great time, but it isn't with them. I feel like it's always with me. I'm never not there. Do you know what I mean? I mean – how about you?'

I feel wrong-footed here because I want to give him a truthful answer but I don't know what that might be. I almost say, 'Those people aren't in the equation.' I almost say, 'I grew up in a house of mistakes.' Both true, but too senten-tious, self-regarding. I say:

'It's not with me, thank God. But I do always cry when I watch *Mary Poppins*, so maybe that means something.'

He doesn't know if I'm joking. I'm not, for the record.

'Don't Go Breaking My Heart' comes on the jukebox and I say:

'I want this played at my funeral.'

That's a line I always say about this song: no one thought it was funny before, except Donna, of course. I've already told him about her. He has a friend who looks out for him too.

He says, 'Zeke strokes my hair when I'm drunk, saying "Lord what do I do to myself?"'

Now I tell him how last summer Donna and I always used to sing this song at karaoke. Rockingham's Piano Bar on Tuesday nights.

'You like karaoke?' he says. 'That's kind of surprising.'

I don't see why he'd think that.

'Damn straight,' I say, 'don't you? It's ace.'

He looks at me and smiles. His teeth seem really white to me, because I'm not used to being around non-smokers I suppose.

'I absolutely love karaoke. It's all about vanity, isn't it? I think it says something about people if they can't do it.'

I'm with him on that one. I went to Rockingham's with James once and all he did was steal a songbook, slipping the red vinyl folder into his rucksack when everyone else was dancing. He thought it was a good 'found object', the photocopied lists of songs and numbers: an encyclopaedia of modern emotion. James could never sing in there, though.

'I'm always getting naked, too,' Newton says. 'I'm sure everyone's had enough of it. It's really not news anymore. The night before I met you I was sitting in the bar in the venue after our gig in Nottingham, naked except for my shirt and socks. And at Hallowe'en, back home, I was naked except I wrapped myself up in clingfilm, with these plastic duckies kind of wrapped up too. I was ducks trapped under the ice. I mean people laughed but I think mainly they were thinking, you know, *why?* . . . is he naked *again?* But it's that same thing, all about getting rid of the vanity, being honest . . . So I was talking to my drummer Gary today about you, and about this girl Renée, this girl that I'm not *dating* per se.' He does finger quotes for dating. He goes on, 'And he was agreeing with me that I should definitely finish with her because I already cheated on her twice.'

'Not including me,' I say. I rub my hand on my chest, and leave it there, by my throat.

'Not including you.'

Big eyes all round. I get up to get more drinks in. When I come back he smiles unsurely, takes a swig of his whisky and lemonade and then goes on:

'It's just that, I feel like last night I remembered how to be with a woman and just meeting you makes a lot of what I've been doing seem meaningless.'

He said that. Who says things like that? No one does but he just did. My mind is racing. But now my face feels like concrete, with my expression just draped over. It's a funny feeling. My mum used to say, 'Take that face off, it's like the sword of Damocles hanging over me.' This conversation seems doomed. He keeps bringing up all these names.

'And then there's Merry, she's so fun and pretty, but . . . I can't make myself really care about her either . . .'

I stretch out my legs and tap my ballet shoes together. They're scuffed so badly the toes look like grey cardboard. I stare at them and press my lips together while he keeps on talking about how faithless he's been, he's *being*, I suppose.

Why do I feel like this, I'm trying to figure out; he's paying me compliments, he's saying this is different, that's the point he's making, isn't it? I keep saying in my mind *I don't know what to do.* The words dissolve there into a queer wonder-feeling of total aloneness while now I'm pulling some face that's breeziness or academic interest and we both have a hold of our stupid small beakers, the mixers flat and the ice cubes thinning and brittle. My mouth feels sealed. My thoughts are getting slippy. He hates being alone. Alone as opposed to what? I imagine him cutting his fingers on the tangle of their doll's hair, caught like bird feet in fishing line.

The jukebox clunks and a new song starts:

They say that you're a runaround lover . . .

Newton grins and frowns and points up at the tiny mounted speaker with an expression that says, How do they *know* this? Who *are* these people . . . ?

I raise an eyebrow and smile but now all I can think is that the dignified thing is to leave. If I wasn't so wretched. If I had any self-respect. My heart beats faster, trips up on itself; at the thought that I could just stand up and walk out.

The feeling throbs in my throat until my head swims. But I don't move. Because how can I leave a room that he's in? *Come on*, How could I ever leave a room that he's in? So I keep widening my eyes and whistling at each new sneaky sin he's speaking about. All these fun and pretty girls he's trotting out for me to look at. But I can't look. What would Mary do? She wouldn't care. She would if she was in love. I know nothing about that word. Do I? I look at him and I have these intimations – in the flicker between us now when I even dare look up from the coin I keep spinning – intimations of what it would be like to come up against somebody commensurate; a calm feeling that I wouldn't care how bloody that battle got. I really wouldn't. But I find I can't speak out with dreams like that wadding my throat. Plus there are these other intimations, these flashes, of what I'd feel when he stopped looking at me like he wanted to know. It might be happening already. So I really shouldn't look again.

I could take his hand and tell him *shhh* . . . But I look over at his free hand, pressing down on the patchy green velour of our seat, on the gummy black bald patches, his knuckles pale and those grubby fingers too pink. My own empty hand – well, there it is – holding on to the edge of the table. Here we are. And I can't break through or out of myself enough. He shrugs and smiles, then gets up to go to the toilet. He stumbles over a badly gaffer-taped rip in the carpet. I would pretend I hadn't seen but, really, there's so much bonhomie flying around that I find myself letting out a failed little high-pitched laugh. It sounds so horrible. I feel so sick at myself, and so grateful that I don't see his face when he hears that. As he pushes the door to the Gents I say out loud what I've kept thinking:

'This is heartbreaking.'

The landlady looks up from her magazine with blank eyes. I fold a beer mat on the edge of the dinted copper table. Tonight feels very old.

Still, we wind up checking in to a hotel. The Gladstone, a grim grey tower a short and silent walk away from the pub. Newton leaves his wallet open on the reception desk while his card's getting swiped and there, in a cracked plastic window, is a black and white photo of him and a girl. A beautiful girl – let's not shy away from saying that. I look for a second. He wants me to look, I guess, so I look. She has a heavy fringe and one sleepy eye shut and an arm around his shoulder. He is goofing off looks like, as per, and seems a good few years younger. Not as tired looking. Vaguely shaved and with something like a haircut. I look away and, aside from what I feel, whatever I feel, imagine that, someone having a picture of you in their wallet years later. It's a great thing, really. I see it and feel sorry I was sulking.

I sit up on the melamine desk in our stuffy, low-ceilinged room and he takes his checked coat off and hangs it on the back of the door before coming over and putting the scratchy heels of his hands on my neck. He kisses me then we just hug for ages. I feel his one warm hand on my back, his other pressing on my neck. He moves them down to my hips and I hold on to the belt loops at the back of his cord jeans and look back into his sleepy lidded, deep brown eyes. It's too much for me. I have to twist my head to look out of the window. Through the grey net I see the club we can hear: two girls leave arm in arm and zigzag down the wet, shining street. The mural on the plywood awning shows garish balloon-bellied cartoon pigs humping each other. I have to look away from that. Newton puts his chin on my shoulder.

'Won't you believe I've been a monster?' he says, so quietly. I have to close my eyes.

I'm watching the rain glazing the window as a slimy grey projection on the faded Regency wallpaper. Newton is face down on my ribs, huffing out his sweet breath, lying between my drawn-up legs, his heartbeat a slowing thud stuck on my belly. I look down at the top of his head, the thick hair lying where my bra is flipped up. First off I feel nothing. I study the whole situation and just don't. Then a little snap in my stomach and I don't know what. Like cold little hands inside pressing out. I squeeze shut my eyes for a dizzy moment. When I open them he rolls his head over a little and says:

'Are you comfortable?'

'I'm fine,' I say.

My hair is damped into chiffon veils. I smooth them out of my face then just stay still.

He sits back on his thighs then and rubs his forehead with the heel of one hand. I twitch my eyes over his eyes, nose, mouth, all in grainy grey and black. He's staring at me.

He says, 'Listen,' and looks up and to the side

and squeezes half of his face up. He blinks and looks back at me, says, 'I've never been like this with anyone before.'

I look at him with my face blank, and after a moment I say, 'Well. Me neither. So.'

I turn my head on the cold pillow, on the stiff cold cotton. He moves to lie down next to me and I stare into the clear dark. When his breathing sounds steadier I turn over and lean on my elbows. He's lying on his back: he has his eyes gently shut and his head on one side. I wait some more, kneeling with the sheet tugged round my legs and the car lights from outside scrolling across us both. Then I put my hands under the twisted covers and press the palms of my hands down hard on his hips so they nudge right in. Looking at him then I get this wishbone feeling down inside, a stretching, a tension, and my heart makes this tripped-up noise, it feels unmoored. I lay down on my back again, close my eyes and stay as still as I can for a long time. Then, keeping my eyes shut, I turn carefully and put my arm round him, squeeze where the scurfy skin slides over his ribs. He does it back to me, the same. He's warm, another person.

In the morning he's off down South with his

band, but before he leaves to meet them he comes to the station with me. There's half an hour until my train, so we go in the busy greasy spoon under the concourse. We haven't spoken much this morning. I feel agitated until the waitress brings over our food: two breakfasts sliding on bin-lid-sized plates. I finish mine too fast while Newton's just picking at his, raking his fork through the beans, shunting an under-done potato cake through a slurp of brown sauce again and again.

'I really don't eat lately,' he says. 'I've been living on ice cubes, pretty much,' he smiles and I smile. I don't think we know what to do. 'But that's quite an impressive appetite you have,' he says as I wipe some spongy toast around the last bits of food. I push the plate aside so I can lean up on my elbows.

'Don't worry. I'm going to go and puke it all up later,' I say, and just look off at the faded out, underwater blue Milk for Life poster on the chipboard wall. He thinks I'm being droll. I don't want to look at him. I don't know what's going on. I don't know what I'm playing at. I start counting the floor tiles, then I smear our linking cup rings on the red table which is covered in crumbs and shiny greasy marks. With each out-breath my skin tightens more with the cold in here. I look up at him looking down at his food. I feel my mouth twitch and look away. Don't think I can stand how his ashy-brown hair falls; how his fingers come out from that frayed coat cuff to hold the knife he's not using.

So I move his plate aside too. And I take his hand and we fiddle with each other's cold hands and don't say a word. I think he's looking at me but I just can't look back at the moment. There's something here I need to take a hold of, but I don't know the first thing about how to.

And then he leans against the wall, away from me, you see, just outside Lime Street.

He says, 'Have you noticed how sometimes you say a lot, and sometimes you really don't?'

It's like it used to be when I was a kid: my mouth is a straight line crossing things out. I shrug.

I say, 'Umm . . .'

And see if I can say something with my eyes instead. We're both thinking the same thing, possibly, it goes back and forth between our eyes. But, no, we're not.

'I think my problem is that I want to fall in love too much,' he says. He squeezes up one side of his face and puts his head on one side.

He's smiling. The chilly morning sun shows up all the age in his face.

My face feels frozen. My dress is being blown sideways by the wind, twisting into helter-skelter creases round my middle. I look down for a while to straighten it.

'Oh. Well. You're the opposite of me then,' I say. I don't know why I say that. I don't think it's especially true.

'I've had my eyes opened to a few things over these last few days,' he says. 'It's going to take me a while to recover and to make sense . . .'

I nod. But we're looking at the space above each other's shoulders by this point. So I think that I may as well fuck things up if they're fucking up.

'Me too,' I say. 'You see, the thing about me is – and now you're really going to think I'm a freak.' I roll my eyes and smile. It probably looks nothing like a smile. 'I hadn't had sex for two years before the other night.'

He nods too, too quickly like he hasn't heard me at all. I look at my hands. My face is blank but I'm thinking *Well there you have it, Newton. You can put your face in the plate and eat that.*

We walk inside slowly and he looks up at the flickering departure board.

'I guess that is kind of a long time,' he says. His hands are in his pockets. He's not looking at me.

I shrug. At the end of my platform he locks his hands behind his head and looks at his shoes. Green Converse, white ribbed socks slumped above them, grey cord painter jeans. I taste his jumper when we hug. His greasy hair feels cold to touch. But then I look back at his feet when I say, so fast I doubt he catches it:

'Yeah, well, maybe we'll meet again some day I certainly was very smitten with you for a while there okay.'

A great speech from Esther and all delivered *without even looking in his eyes*. He cups my face in his hands quickly now and kisses me again and again. Kisses me, but I turn my head away and frown and *shake his hand* now when all I want to do is shake his shoulders, smash my mouth back on to his because, Jesus, how often do you get to look into eyes like that? The answer is you don't. You never, never do. And I avoid them. And then I turn and give my ticket in and walk along the platform and do nothing but listen to my flat feet thud. Is he watching me go or has he turned and left already? I have a ridiculous expression on my face. I want to turn around and look. I think *Now. Now. Now.* But I keep on paddling straight ahead and I get on the train at the first door I come to. I hit the open button and yawn into my sleeve, already trying to convince myself that these are shrill, thin emotions I'm feeling. I can tear them up and the shreds won't last, won't hold on, they'll dissolve.

8

I thought I wanted to walk home, but I find I don't have the energy, so I go to the bus stop. In Piccadilly Gardens the rock kids are all acting casual – sitting hunched on the lawns asking each other who's here and who's coming. They pull up their jersey hoods against the sharp wind, which quivers the stiff branches of all the decorative saplings that are stabbed into tiny squares of earth amongst the benches. Pigeons cut up the blank sky.

Upstairs on the bus I sit in the last empty double seat. The thin air is dank and there's a breathy grey film on the windows. There's the smell of worn-out mint gum and of sweet shampoo, from the girl in front of me who is combing her wet blonde hair out over and over. I watch her and I don't think about anything. Then I watch a puddle of spilt drink in the aisle elongating with the acceleration, licking at a screwed-up sweet wrapper as the bus heaves itself away from a stop.

A man huffs his way upstairs: fifty-odd, in a striped shirt, a leather jacket. He stands in the aisle mouth-breathing with one hand tight on the smeared metal banister. Everyone with a free seat next to them looks absorbed in themselves and the windows they can't see out of. When he sits down I move just enough so our legs aren't touching, that's all. I close my eyes and lean my head against the damp glass. He nudges me as he struggles to take his bomber jacket off. The grey leather squeaks. He's all elbows. I can smell his sweat spreading. I try and get engrossed in an excitable phone conversation on the seat behind me. With my eyes still closed I lift my eyebrows and press my lips together when the he-said she-said prompts. I breath in time with a baby's crooning crying downstairs. But I have to move up again, a little, because his leg keeps pressing mine and I can feel his soft flesh through the fabric, shifting. Can hear a ticking noise, too. He presses against me *again* and I'm going to just get up and go and stand downstairs, but then I look round at him. Down at him.

'*Jesus. Fuck's sake,*' I say. I shoo him off, tutting, 'Go away. Get off the bus, you fuck. Go on.'

He gets up. He looks at me with sulky little

boy eyes before he goes back down the stairs. He doesn't say anything. I can't imagine his voice. People look round. Someone laughs. People tell people what happened. I press my hands flat against the seat in front and put my head forward.

At an old man's stall by the bus stop I buy a squashy pear, its skin blooming with traffic soot. I rub it on my anorak and eat it as I walk home. My fingers and wrist get wet from the thin juice twirling down. My hand feels freezing. My shoe ribbons are trailing. Up ahead, the wind keeps snatching at a stray sheet of newspaper, tugging it along the pavement, lifting it high then letting it drop. I watch as I walk along, and wince as I get closer because it flaps upwards as if jerked on a string, coming right at me. What to do? I duck a little but still it touches my head as it floats over. I close my eyes and when I open them I meet the gaze of this red-haired scruff who's trailing his bike towards me: a swaggerer, a pop-and-crisps kid.

'Means you're special,' he says.

Newton has left two things to prove he existed. A letter on my pillow; I knew there'd be one. It's written in blue ballpoint on the back of one of my scribblings. There's an address on the bottom, and a phone number. It's sad that while I read it I know it's from before, that it's basically meaningless now. I should mention that I've not thrown it away though, for whatever that's worth. Maybe I'll mention too that it's folded up in my wallet in my cardigan pocket, for whatever that's worth. I tell Donna what I did about his other calling card, when she gets in from work.

'You did what?'

She can't speak through laughing. She cackles and jumps on my bed and off it again. I hear those old springs ping and the dust puffs out. She runs round me then sits up on one of the box towers.

'What did you do? Mix it with rose petals and eyelashes and spread it on toast.'

I grin and shake my head. 'No,' I say, 'it was more homeopathic.'

Donna keeps talking, shaking her head. 'You toxic witch.'

I shrug. 'It's romantic. That's romance, Donna. Take note.' I tap the side of my nose and nod.

'I'm just picturing you pouring it in,' Donna says, staring at me.

I sit down by her, close my eyes and lean back

against the bed, say, 'Are you? That's nice.' I do my mum's voice: 'You always go too far, don't you?'

Donna makes two beaks with her tiny hands and snaps along. We give each other the giggles. I have tears all over my face and I keep getting a stitch. I'm in such a good mood I can't stand it. I feel like I've just pulled off something amazing. That kind of precarious joy, when you think you're finally in the clear.

We move to the kitchen to get some tea. I sit up on the counter and while she makes it I say:

'Let me tell you about this guy . . . His skin looked like a mouldy old flannel, his nose was squashed, and covered in blackheads, he had this big ursine belly and a sweaty, sunken chest. Dirty hands, sulky eyes, I mean, he was gorgeous. He was it.'

'This is weird,' Donna says. 'You don't even like ursine men, you like . . . what's the word for ferrets? So, is he still in the country?'

'Yes, but he flies back tomorrow, to Vermont.'

'Vermont,' she says. 'All I know about Vermont is . . .'

'Yeah, Salinger's holed up there,' I say.

She nods.

'Robert Frost is buried there,' I say.

She clicks her fingers. 'And Donna Tartt went to college there.'

'The other Donna,' I say.

I don't tell her much about Liverpool, but I do show her my letter. She reads it slowly and then looks at me. She's convinced I should contact him. She decides I should go and see him, in fact, make the bold move. So I see myself twirling my heels on some candy-coloured clapboard house doorstep, listening to the bell ring inside, buffing my fingernails on my lapels. What his face will do and what will mine be doing? But it's a cheap daydream. However breathless I make myself now, I know I'm too late.

'His favourite film's *The Graduate*, maybe he'd appreciate the grand gesture,' I say, 'but I think he's reached the same conclusion I have on this one.'

'You'd be pleased if he showed up here one day, wouldn't you,' she says.

'Of course. But he won't.'

'Well, some people are so scared they will just walk away if you give them half a chance to.'

'Yep,' I say. 'Me.'

'Call him. Treat it as an exercise in . . . narrative fulfilment.'

'What it as a what in what?' I say.

'Yeah,' she says.

'Well, no, I don't need that. That's what the TV is for,' I say and draw a box with my index fingers.

Donna puts down her mug, puts her fists on her hips and ums and ahs.

I say, 'No – this can be a nice loose end floating.'

I lean back and mime loose-end-floating with both hands.

'Like Isadora Duncan's scarf,' Donna says. Then she stops pacing and sits down too.

'I can't do anything, Donna, it'd be a risky venture, when I'm okay with myself now.'

'Not from this rocking chair, sister,' she says. She flicks the zip on her cardigan and rolls her head back for a moment, then she looks at me. 'Oh, call him.' She bangs the table with the flat of her hand, smiles a cross-toothed smile and says, 'What's the worst that could happen?'

That makes me petrified, makes me feel ice cold. The worst that could happen. It would be the least successful phone call in the history of creation. I imagine my laden Hello and his voice thin, cheery, indifferent.

'Donna, stop it,' I say, 'stop it.' I look at her to show I mean it.

Now she's leaning forward in her seat, with her eyes shining and an unsure smile.

'I'm sure his life's not like mine. He probably has hobbies, a personal life. So he doesn't need me throwing pebbles at his bedroom window. "When people fall in love with love they fling themselves in the abyss." I read that once.'

'Yeah, and?' she says.

'It's okay. I'm young, the world's huge, he's just one person. I'll forget him.'

'Esther, people fall in love with one person. It's not hysterical to think it happened to you. I think both our bookshelves will testify it's a well-documented phenomenon.'

'Well, it's very pretty to think so, but I don't think that's what they testify at all. Not at all,' I say. 'You're tickling me into liking the idea, but it's a recipe for self-loathing. I can't do it. Anyway, I'd get there and that address would be a . . . Dunkin' Donuts, then what?'

We both say it at the same time in the same way: 'Have a fucking donut.'

Donna rubs her face and looks right at me. 'If it happened like you're telling me then it's the only honest thing to do, you've got no *choice* really. Did it happen like you're saying?'

I think so. I don't know. She looks at me and I kind of shrug while I'm nodding.

'There isn't really a problem here,' she says. 'What aren't you telling me?'

'I'm an open book,' I say, looking away. This is an old routine between us.

'Yeah, by bloody Jean Rhys.'

'Hardly,' I say. I talk out of the window, at the murky sunset, with all these awkward sudden fears in my stomach. 'I realised what I felt was new. You know my opinion of religion, but I looked in his eyes and felt like building a cathedral with my bare hands. Then he started telling me all about his exes and girls he knocks about with. It sounds like he waves his dick around like a plastic sword. Which is fine, I know, that's neither here nor there, but the subtext was: *don't think you're special*, anyway, I'm not going to sit here and rake over the nuances. You know how I act. You know me.'

Her face isn't nice to look back at now because she does know me.

'The world isn't my playground,' I say.

'No, Esther, and thank God. Don't you think I'm serious? I am. Call him. This doesn't happen every day, you know.'

Of course I know. But I'm not going to make

some self-defeating phone call. I stand up to act it out:

'Hi, is that Newton? Hey there. Hi. Esther. *Esther*. Manchester Esther? Yeah. Oh, not so bad . . . bit of typing, you know, paperwork . . . *In vain have I struggled . . .*'

'Forget that,' Donna says; she's laughing at me and squinting at me. 'It's "Get your party pants on. Esther's coming to town." Shy people always confuse each other. He wouldn't say that stuff if he didn't mean it; it's pointless.'

'Listen, Donna,' I say. I look at my hands while I tell her the score, and I can feel my face getting twisted and burning and ugly while I do. 'He said it because he could see what I am. I *stink* of loneliness.' I flash my eyes up for a second, 'I know I do. I walk in a room and the atmosphere curdles. I make people's flesh crawl when they see the look in my eyes. I make my own flesh crawl. He just saw that probably, saw that whatever he said to me I'd be on like piranhas, and I was, I really was.'

I nod at that and kind of laugh. Then I can't speak anymore. I have to press my mouth on to the back of my hand for a second. My teeth are all clenched up.

I force down a deep breath and then say,

'Being lonely is the worst reason to do anything, least of all tip yourself in someone's lap, and I feel so lonely that I just want to howl. So.'

She leans back in her chair and looks at me then down at her forearm, which she scratches. Then we both watch through the window the bent over old man from across the street come out of his house and drop a carrier bag of rubbish in his bin before getting into his red car and driving off.

'Do you remember,' Donna says, taking her half-moon glasses off and polishing them on her cardigan, 'I always carried that copy of *Howl* about with me, when I was fourteen? Everywhere I went. That battered old hardback copy that my . . .'

'What?' I throw up my hands.

'What?' She grins and widens her eyes.

'Is this a conversation or a word association game?' I stand up. 'Jesus.'

Donna stares up. 'Christ,' she says, 'and now I've talked myself into a verbal cul-de-sac.'

She stares at me. I just nod a lot and suck air through my teeth, still staring out of the window.

I say, 'And then *leapt* behind a privet . . .'

She takes the legendary snow globe off the windowsill and shakes it.

9

But when I try to float down to the truth of what I'm feeling, I find I can't do it. There's no natural law, and when I lie still and let go it's only to find myself struggling in that suspense, through sleepless nights where it's too easy to set my heart thudding, to make myself sweat; but where there's nothing to kick against, just a limitless darkness where I don't know what I'm inventing.

One morning last week Donna knocked on my door before she went to work and said:

'Rise and shine, Raskolnikov.'

I kept my face to the wall and curled up tighter and growled at her. The door wasn't locked though so she came in with a cup of tea for me. I poked my bare backside out from the duvet.

She said, 'Yes, officer, I recognise that face.' And laughed to herself all the way down the hallway.

Today wasn't so good. When she said, 'Morning Marcel,' and came on in I was half soused already, swaddled in my duvet on the floor. Donna stared at me and so I stared back.

Then I looked down. She took the bottle off the bedside table and emptied it over my head. The gin burnt my eyes and felt sticky and it stank, but for a long time I didn't get up to wash it off. I lay back, in fact, closed my eyes and half enjoyed being a rancid Ophelia. I have to ham it up because how I feel is difficult, that's all.

Donna wasn't around for me to pester last night and I didn't feel like reading or writing. My mind was doing its own thing, so sometime after three I switched on the portable at the bottom of my bed. With the volume turned right down and the colour muted to a bleary glow it was my small, grubby window on the world. Something had happened somewhere cold: I watched exhilarated eyewitnesses shaking their heads and gesticulating with gloved hands; hair blowing in their faces; fires raging behind them. I pointed my big toe to switch channels, to a game show, with a glamorous girl turning clunky lit letter blocks around to form catch-phrases. Those half-hidden sentences kept holding mistaken meanings for me, but I blinked and they were gone. I tried hard to follow that, but in the moments when the screen blanked after an ad break my room was silent and dark and then I really started to panic, looking across at the moon glinting in the empty mirror. I got up and sat by my speakers, played some records with my headphones on and had some drinks. I didn't hear Donna come in.

After she left today I went to the window and watched her drive off. Leaves were twitching on the pink twigs outside my window, the blossom was shivering. Then, when the wind coursed, the white petals scattered and stormed, careering down our road, sticking to the dirty car roofs and the lampposts, joining the choco-late wrappers and the chip papers on the oily pavement.

I had a bath and went out. Halfway to town I started to feel really ill. My hair was wet and dripping cold water round my neck, down my back. I felt freezing and sweaty at the same time. I was sick against a wall behind an office, on a pile of baby-blue, butterfly-knotted carrier bags which were spilling shredded paper on a pave-ment already stained dark. I leant over, held my own hair back and poured it all out. I didn't feel too good about that. I wiped my mouth on my anorak sleeve then went and lay back on a bench behind the cathedral. I was shivering and my heart was pounding. I stared up at the palled sky for an hour or so, until the films started, then I spent the rest of the daylight hours in the multiplex: half lying down, with the armrests switched up; concentrating hard, trying hard to get carried away.

Now it's late and Donna's out rehearsing and I'll need some help sleeping. I walk round to the corner shop for a bottle of gin. I put ice in my glass and take it with me. When I get back I get into bed with my clothes still on. I opened one of my boxes last week. I felt like rereading the books I liked when I was a kid, the stories I know inside out: *Anne of Green Gables*, *Wuthering Heights, Frankenstein*. I flip-flop about on the bed reading them in the evenings, trying hard to fall asleep sober with their old smell on the pillow next to me.

Tonight I find *Moby Dick*. Donna borrowed it during our initial Billy Rocker marine frenzy. I turn to the last page because her bookmark is still in there. It's one of the postcards she sent him, a montage of Manchester's municipal heritage: the Town Hall, Central Library's sooty portico and a flat, dun-coloured airport terminal. All she's written on it is HERE BE MONSTERS. I prop it up on the bedside table and go back to the book. Donna's put her red line under this:

The drama's done. Why then does anyone step forth? Because one did survive the wreck.

And lower down, my blue pen boxes a fragment:

her retracing search after her missing children, only found another orphan.

The card was addressed to Lisbon. Billy Rocker was causing trouble on that peninsula sometime last year if I remember rightly. He's been neglecting Donna of late. I wonder where he is now? I open the window and finish my drink with the cold coming in. I hold my empty glass to one eye like a telescope, see bleeding stars through the melting ice.

Today – Sunday – is Donna's only day off for the foreseeable so I go out early, past the post office to the corner shop for some papers. I leave most of them on the doormat; shake out the supplements for the neighbours to scrap over. We don't need that material in our flat.

Donna's en route to the bathroom when I get back, glinting down the hallway in her moon-shiny silk pyjamas. Her hair looks frightening and her face is out of focus.

I say, 'What have I told you about the evils of drink.'

She looks confused. She says, 'Elvis. Drink.' And gives me two thumbs up. Her eyelids are fluttering.

She comes into the kitchen after her shower and sits down for a tea and toast symposium.

As we read our fingers get smudged and sooty, and soon her clean glowing face has fingerprints all over it from how she sits with her hands holding her head up. There's newsprint in her hairline. I'm doing the crossword when she swivels a page she's reading around to face me, and, good grief, there's my mum. A huge photo. Some article about second marriages.

'Christ, what's she thinking?' I say.

Donna shrugs and laughs, turns the page back round.

'Silly woman,' I say.

We keep reading. I keep seeing my mum's face there.

When my phone starts pipping, right on cue, I tell Donna who it will be, and when I show her the number on the screen, the Liverpool code, she rolls her eyes. I forget that he exists, so seeing that gives me that same weary feeling I used to get watching his bulk shifting behind our old frosted-glass front door on a Saturday morning, or, later, hearing his car horn being leant on in our cul-de-sac.

'Hello there, it's your dad,' he says. He asks what I'm doing with myself these days.

'Not much, bit of typing,' I say.

'Oh. Hm. Have you seen your brother?'

'No.'

'Where's he living?'

'I couldn't tell you to be honest.'

'What's that word you used?'

'Estranged. Yes, we're still estranged. He's still strange.'

'Why are you in a temper?' he says. 'Has another one dumped you?' He laughs, then sounds like he is about to say goodbye.

'Well,' he says, 'just thought I'd check up on you.'

Then,

'Oh, did you see your mother in the paper today?'

'Yeah.'

'It was a weird thing. I've had the newspaper lying open on my living-room floor all morning on that page and I didn't recognise her. I just thought it was an appropriate photo for the article: a woman with this look of *slight insecurity* on her face. I also thought this woman had an abnormally long neck. Then your uncle Ernest rang and said, "Have you seen the *Observer*?" and I said yeah, but I still didn't click. He came round at lunchtime and pointed it out and I was like, so? Because my first thought was just, Why has this woman got such a long neck? Did her boyfriend arrange that? Does he know people in journalism?'

'Her husband, no, I presume they advertised for people . . .'

'Why is the picture so big?' he says.

'It's not that big.'

'She's standardised her bloody looks, hasn't she? She's gone blonde, like all other bloody women.'

'She's gone grey. It's a black and white photo.'

'Oh. I'll have another look. It's in the bathroom. Just the neck, looks so weird.'

'Not really,' I say. Dad, I keep thinking, Don't.

'Cartoon-long.'

'Right.'

'It's just such a bloody odd photo, that's all.'

I say nothing. I hold the phone so Donna can hear too. We wiggle eyebrows at each other.

'It's like a *goose's* neck,' he says.

'No it's not.'

A pause.

'*You'll* end up like that,' he says. His voice goes up.

I roll my eyes at Donna, who just shakes her head and looks at her hands.

'Fine,' I say.

He fails at laughing then.

'They're a constant disappointment, aren't they?' Donna says after we've said goodbye. I don't know what to say. My dad's not as bad as he was, at least. When my brother and I were very young, we were at the old house with him one weekend and he turned the television off and sat down to tell us very seriously that he'd got a job in Australia. He hadn't. He wanted to see if we'd want to go with him. We didn't. A year or so after I left home he tracked me down and faked a cancer scare to make me return his calls. But the most bizarre incident was when I was thirteen, and I stopped going on Saturdays and he rang and told me he knew my mum was keeping me away from him. I remember him telling me that, on the phone. He said, 'Your mother's accusing me of sexual abuse, you know.' And I said 'Sexual?' I can hear myself saying it.

I was sitting on the stairs. My mum wasn't stopping me going, I'd made that decision myself. I wanted to hang out with Donna instead. I'd had one of my glorious tantrums about it. I locked myself in the bathroom and sat under the sink with my eyes in the crook of my bent back elbow trying to concentrate on the sound of running water. Blood was beating in my face, my mum was tapping on the door and my brother was shouting at her not to fucking bother. Donna never had these problems. She was lucky that way. No, I really shouldn't say that.

We have a nice morning together today: reading all the papers through, chewing our pens and sipping our tea. By lunchtime all the reports look like all our books: the columns runged with underlinings; scribbled stars and question marks tumbling down the margins.

I tore another page off the kitchen calendar today. And I decided it's time to roll off this sick bed, to roll up my trousers and let another summer of lushdom commence; put in a few hours attractively wrecking my looks. Such as they are. I wink at myself in the mirror after my bath.

I put on my prairie dress over my jeans, with Donna's Converse, and my hair plaited up with a Biro in it. As I walk into town I do something I haven't done for a while and start taking shallower and shallower breaths, speeding up until the air – smelling of hops from the Boddington's factory, of the diesel from a bus chuffing at the junction – feels like it's being pulled in by itself. In one beat I drop my shoulders, let them swing some and slow down. I jump off the kerb and up again and have a couple of puffs on an invisible cigarette. A gang of pigeons shatter their shadows over the railway bridge. A vinyl builders' sign pinned between windows above an ex-restaurant floats free of its taut corners to show a dead neon scrawl, saying *Monsoon Nights*. When I crouch to tie a lace that's been trailing through old puddles I see how the setting sun is making sparks of the hairs on my ankles.

Saturday night in the bar, and Donna is ministering to the misunderstood as per. The boy taking money on the door seems to be asleep. He's folded up with his forehead on the till so I can't see his face. All the old inmates of this ghost ship are present and correct. Lots of people – men – alone and one full table near the back: six loudmouths all shaking their heads and shouting over one another.

Barbara Ann is working tonight as well – she's the girl I first saw in here with Mary that night when I met that Newton. Her hair is streaked with blonde, now. There's no customers want serving so she's doing the wa-watusi by the bottle skip. As I lean over the bar to give my bag to Donna a familiar Mr Pitiful on the stool next door but one pipes up. Everything's a rather glum melodrama with this fellow. He'd pour his heart out to me for half an hour if he'd bought the wrong toothpaste. Now he tells me,

'I've got a bottle of whisky at home. Why do

you think I've trekked out into town at half past
ten?'

Donna leans on the bar and tilts her head to
one side, says, 'Well, why don't you tell us about
it?'

'Because I'm lonely and it's all my own doing.'

She fills up his glass and gets me a gin. He's
lonely. One side of his face is plush and pink with
the lights on it, the other is pulled down in steely
shadows. Mine looks just the same, no doubt.

He lays down his head.

'His problem is he thinks he's Frank Sinatra
reincarnated,' I say. Donna puts her thumbs in
her jeans' belt loops and nods slowly.

'Frank Sinatra was one talented son of a bitch,'
she says, then starts wiping the bar with a stringy
grey flannel. I watch it moving back and forth
and around. The fan's not working and it's deadly
hot and sticky.

'My eyes are sweating,' I say.

'Oh. Song title. Let me write that down. Give
me your pen, come on.'

'Is it too late to tell you the sarcasm doesn't
suit you, Donna?'

I slump over and sigh.

'What can I do,' Donna says. 'Tell me and I'll
do it.'

I raise my eyes but keep my head down when I say, 'No. I'm alright. Worse things happen at sea. Speaking of which. How's your pen pal?'

Her eyes glint at that. 'Do you want to hear the latest letter?'

I sit up and I nod.

'I have something else to show you,' she says, then disappears under the bar.

I hoist myself up to watch her crawl behind where the boxes of cans are stacked. I see her feet twitching then she emerges with a red face, a grazed arm, and the fat green cardboard folder all the mail is kept in. She flicks through the bills and prize draw offers and then says:

'Here we go: love and squalor from the Scottish Amazon.'

She hands me a homemade postcard. An intricate decoupage collage: the Eiffel Tower being strangled by strange flowers. The back just says:

M. x.

The last time I saw Mary she had a stack of different coloured envelopes on her kitchen table, addressed to her last half-dozen lovers. I didn't ask what was in them, but she was smiling very smugly to herself when she picked them up to post on her way to the airport. Donna coughs and I look up. She pushes her damp fringe out of her face then polishes her shoes – my shoes – on the back of her jeans, Left then Right. The sheaf of thick, cream paper she's holding is franked with cup rings. Billy Rocker's in Japan now.

She reads out what he says,

DEAREST DONNA,
SAILING IS A LONELY LIFE. I WAS THINKING ABOUT YOU LAST NIGHT AND I FELL INTO AN INTERMINABLE BROWN STUDY ON THE POOP DECK. I JUST WISH I COULD HAVE BROUGHT YOU WITH ME IN MY DUFFEL BAG. THE SKY IS CLEAR. THE SEA LOOKS LIKE THE ONE ON YOUR GRANDMA'S PLATES. THERE'S NOT MUCH TO DO HERE BUT LOOK GUILTY, AND THE ANSWER TO EVERY QUESTION IS, 'OF COURSE I HAVE. I'M A SAILOR . . .' LET'S NOT DWELL ON THAT. I HAVE SOME QUESTIONS OF MY OWN. I ADDRESS THEM TO THE NIGHT SKY SOMETIMES. MAYBE I SHOULD ADDRESS THEM TO YOU INSTEAD. I SUSPECT YOUR

ANSWERS WOULD BE PITHIER. IN THE MEANTIME I KNOW YOU'LL BE KEEN TO HEAR ABOUT THE LATEST ADVENTURES OF THAT LITTLE SMUDGE, MARMITE, THE SHIP'S CAT, WELL . . .

And so on.

Donna grins a cross-toothed grin, shaking her head as she folds the letter back up.

'How ace is Billy Rocker?'

'Yes,' I say, 'a British tar is a soaring soul.'

She's a real gone goose and I should think so too. It's great material. But I could feel what my face was doing while her eyes were twinkling. I was tapping my fingers on my glass and biting my bottom lip when I smiled. I watch Barbara Ann close her eyes and spin slowly on the spot to the Georgie Fame record that's playing. Then I look over at the kid asleep on the door.

'Yeah,' Donna says. 'Dean. He's very enigmatic.'

'Do you mean he's enigmatic or do you mean he's got a long fringe?' I say.

'He does have a long fringe,' she nods. 'And he probably has band badges on his pyjamas. He's only eighteen.'

I down my drink then shake my head and lay

it down on the clipped wings my elbows make
on the bar. I feel my lips touch the sticky marble
tiles. I'm giving myself dingy visions in the
pressing heat, then I know someone has come
to sit next to me when through my closed eyes
I see the sunburst of a match being lit. The bar
is blurred for a moment when I look up. It's
my old friend Joey is sitting next to me. I haven't
seen him in a long time. He's hugging the bar
and sucking on his cigarette, his face as crum-
pled as his tablecloth shirt. His eyes are friendly;
he says Alright Esther and grins and his chin
sticks out. I smile back sleepily.

'How's it going?' he says.

I nod. 'Oh, you know.'

'Yeah, me too,' he says and we both try and
pull a rueful face.

He grips his head with his hands and says,
'Aaargh!' and I laugh with my eyes wide.

We get some more drinks in. He picks up a
shredded slice of lemon from in the ashtray he's
using and holds it up by the spiky string the
flesh is all pulled out into. He swings the crescent of gritted pith and peel between us, twirls
it above us like a mobile for a kid's cot. We both
look up. There's a flash. Donna's taken a photo.

We talk for a while, then Joey stands up.

'I'm going up the road for a few if you fancy. I can feel my soul getting tobacco-stained in here.'

'Yeah, I might come up in a bit,' I say.

He recommends me a record before he goes, takes my pen from my ponytail and writes the title on my arm. I read the unfamiliar hand-writing as I go downstairs: CHORE OF ENCHANTMENT in thin letters stretching, each one taller than the last.

The Ladies is empty. The pipes whinny when I spin the taps. I sit in the middle cubicle, with my feet up on the seat and my chin on my knees. The music upstairs is shuddering through my shoes and my head is resting against the cistern. I'm feeling hyperaware – of my blinking, of my breathing. The flush handle is in my temple and I get to thinking it doesn't need to press too hard and my skull will implode. I begin to wonder if the bone there is any thicker than eggshell. Didn't I read that somewhere?

I'm not moping about Newton here, by the way. That's dead, I promise. Although I guess I could easily make him what I talk about. I could become that kind of wino: garrulous and heart-broken forever. Or there's that other, silent species of drunk, whose sentiments are brittle, whose biliousness has simply evanesced. They're the ones who get shark eyes by the end of the night, looking at everything with these hole-punched, expressionless voids, however friendly they're acting. There's a couple of them upstairs tonight. I don't know why, but I'm lumbered with this idea that Newton and I are both of us awake in the witching hours, busy putting empty bottles in the bin and our autistic fictions of true love out there. Maybe it's true. Maybe he'll let our dalliance drift unsung into the past. For my part I'd like to get it out quick. Then it's not in me anymore. That's a simple equation. Keep swigging the emetic medicine, bring up some sour swill, some glossy drool. I'll tell Donna that one. I look at my overgrown nails: sharp hard things pinching the pen I've pulled out of my ponytail. What about that kid upstairs? *Esther takes a Lover*, there's new ground. I hear footsteps. I call out,

'Any paper over there?'

Donna slides my notebook under the door.

I spit on my fingers to rub off where my mascara's spread. My hair looks wild and streaming. My face is still blotchy, but there's no one to see that in the dark upstairs.

Barbara Ann's clearing up, standing on tiptoe to sweep empty cans off the top of the jukebox. The boy on the door's not moved. He's still asleep on the stool by the till: his arms between his legs, his shoulders and head slumped, an unhooked marionette.

'Same again for me, Donna, and a glass of milk for junior.' I nod towards him then I look right in her eyes. Her mouth twitches.

'I'm going to make him a strong coffee,' she says, 'but okay.'

I put Dean's cup down and cough and he lifts his head up and blinks at me. I introduce myself but it turns out he knows my name already. He shakes his head when he shakes my hand, trying to wake himself up.

Donna's sending Barbara Ann home early. She walks past and grins at us both as she zips up her pink anorak. I smile and Dean says:

'You always look like you're in a bad mood, Esther. When you smile it's really terrific.'

'Okay,' I nod and squint at him. He points at the coffee I've brought.

'When I drink too much of this I feel like I'm glowing in the dark,' he says, then drinks it all in one draught, without wincing. He sits stock-still for a second and then he makes spokey snowflakes with both his hands and frowns at them. He says, 'Hey, Esther, do I look funny to you?'

He does look funny, but not in the way he thinks. It's his swooping blond fringe over his stern eyes, and his small crescent smile under a big turned-up nose. He does look very young. He tells me that he's new in town and has been sleeping on couches.

'Well, I don't have a couch,' I tell him.

After Donna's locked up and paid the bouncer we're all three talking outside, waiting for two taxis. The sky is electric blue behind low clouds. We're all shivering. Dean sits on the ledge next to me, his anorak collar up and his knees up too, ankles crossed. He's wearing scuffed laceless brogues which he tells me he calls his hobo shoes. I find myself imagining that his feet are bare. That he's sitting out with bare feet.

Kissing him would at least be a reason to close my eyes and stop everything. Let the 3 a.m. street sounds in the cold air swirl around me and maybe not think about what happened out here before. But, no, I get in the taxi with Donna. It's overheated in there. The radio's playing slow songs.

'You alright?' Donna asks.

'Yeah, I'm fine,' I say. 'I'm tired. I'm going to do some proper work tomorrow.'

She nods. 'Poor Dean,' she says, 'he's another guitar-afflicted dope.'

'Donna,' I say, 'you're a guitar-afflicted dope.'

'I know it,' she says, and she might be smiling out of the window.

'But on a rainy day I'd take him home,' I say.

Donna draws a breath as if she's going to reply, but she doesn't say anything.

In tribute to Mary I hired out a stack of early Truffaut movies from Central Library yesterday. I hope she's having a good time in Paris, knicker-sniffing. I watched three back-to-back on the portable, smoking my invisible cigarette fiercely all the while, writing things in my detective notebook. Those films have so much life in them – it's upsetting. Each time the action stopped and the snow started I pulled open the curtains and pushed open the window to watch the traffic and swallow cold air.

And you'll forgive me this? I decided it's okay to want company sometimes. So I made a call and tonight Dean is sitting on my bedroom floor with me, next to the speakers, telling me over and over that he's *sunk*. But he's *young*. He keeps nodding forward and swaying back. We've been drinking all day and now the bottle can't find the glass. Earlier, after he got ID'd at the off-licence, we found out we had the same birthday, his two years before mine. On our way back here he kept rubbing his face and then staring at me.

He said, 'Esther – do you not think that's weird?'

'Not really,' I said, but he couldn't get over it. He was shaking his head and frowning.

'Hmm . . .' he said, then, 'Esther: coincidence or conspiracy?'

'Purity or the void?' I said, walking ahead.

He argued with that for a while. I haven't asked where he's from and I can't place the accent, but he has a strange, taut voice, like something that's out of tune. There's a shudder in it, as if he's crushing his Megarider in his pocket and trying not to grind his jaw. He's always huffing and sighing and shaking his slippy fringe. Even the way he breathes sounds effortful; thick-lipped, snot-nosed and tantrum prone. I quite like that though. At least he thinks before he speaks. At least he is sincerely trying to communicate. Better that than these people who have a spiel, whose insights and emotions are nothing more than rodomontade: laughter from the hostages round the table, rolled eyes from the wait staff. No, I would say Dean has a kind of gravitas about him, even when pulling at the neck of his shirt or kicking at the skirting board. He's done a lot of both of those things this evening.

But now, for no good reason, he's decided he needs to go for a walk outside by himself. He shakes himself into his coat, falls over twice. His limbs keep folding up. I'm not too happy about him being at large in the community in that state, now that it's dark, but whatever, out he clatters. I sit in the kitchen and read my Ouspensky. Donna's doing the Russians and passing them on to me. Our quest continues to be Manchester's most tiresome autodidacts. Dean reappears after an hour or so, and in high spirits, too. He tells me he's been lying in the bushes out front thinking. His narrow back bangs into the walls as he walks up the hallway in front of me. There are dissolving dead leaves smeared on the shaved nape of his neck, and on the back of his blue anorak.

We sit on the floor in my room again and I put my arms round him for a bit: one hand stroking his slinky hair, the other one gone dead and tingling, trapped between his head and his shoulder. I kiss his scalding scalp while my mind's elsewhere. I look at my dead hand and flap it stiffly, trying to get the feeling back. When I lean across him to turn the music off he goes very still for a second, says, 'I was listening to that', all muffled there, then looks up with his eyes shut for long enough to say, 'Track six', before he lets his heavy head fall back. So okay. I free my arms, and pop the buttons on his crumply blue shirt, then lay my hands on his cockleshell ribcage. We listen to track six.

Dean has a lot of spare time too, so we start to tag around together. God help me – when I met him this afternoon he was crunching on a lollipop. Standing outside the Odeon, leaning forward and frowning and tugging on the stick. I could taste it when we were – God help me – kissing on the back row: all that vanilla sugar packed into the jagged valleys of his teeth.

After the film we go drinking as usual. The streets get tangled, the whole town seems as drunk as us. We end up in a pub off Dickinson Road where Donna and James and I sometimes used to go. I've been sticking to my gin, but Dean's been pinballing between the pumps and the optics. In here he asks for a pint of bitter.

'You're heading for disaster,' I tell him. 'You're setting sail for shipwreck.'

'Hey, Esther,' he shakes his fringe, 'I have a system going here, trust me.' He pats me on the shoulder and says, 'Trust me.'

There are five old-timers sitting around the polished velvet benches in the snug making music: four with their guitars on their knees, bouncing them up and down and nodding with their eyes closed; one has a washboard and he's singing loudest. When they finish everyone in the pub puts down their nursed drinks to clap. Dean claps hard, and whoops, then he gets up and goes over to ask if he can join in with them. They all say sure, they're a laid-back bunch. A short man with a maroon jumper and salt and pepper hair goes to lean on the bar and Dean sits down and takes up his polished blonde-wood guitar. The dim light glints on it in liquid shapes as he settles it on his knee. He smiles round at everyone before he plays: a slow twelve-bar blues. I watch his hand sweeping the strings. Then he starts up singing.

His voice is thin and creaky,

I've been arrested,

– with his eyes on the floor and his eyebrows pulling together –

I've been arrested,
I know I've done something wrong.

He repeats these lines a fair few times and the old guys join in. Every time I think he's going to sing something new he sings those lines again. It's pretty funny. The man on the washboard nods with his eyes shut and Dean starts swinging his head from side to side. Deep breath. And . . .

I've got Tourette's,

he sings,

I've got Tourette's
Fuck cunt fuck bugger fucking fucking slag moth-
erfucking cunt.

He falls forward over the guitar and starts laughing. His laugh is silent: his small mouth stretches, his eyes roll back. The old-timers are laughing too, I'm glad to say. I have a puff on my invisible cigarette and then buy us both another drink: gin for me, a Baileys for laughing boy.

Dean's pretty fearless. And I always want to kiss him when I'm drunk. The lonely thing is when we're sober. Then I find talking to him is like playing tennis with a racket with no strings. The other night he said to me:

'Do you think we do most of our communicating without talking?'

He didn't think it was a bad thing either, it was just an observation he made. I said:

'Well, recently I just like to talk to the mirror or my belly button.'

He thought about that and frowned into the distance. 'It's good to have a relationship with your body,' he said.

Given that Dean's such a rackety drunk, it's strange that he sometimes freezes up, zones out completely. When we get in tonight I come back from the bathroom to find him sitting folded up against the fridge in our dark kitchen, breathing sleepily and avoiding eye contact. I move one of his thin, flung out arms, sit down next to him on the sticky floor and say his name. No reply. If I cared I imagine I would tear myself up trying to get one kind word or look out of him, make him squeeze my hand back at least.

But I don't care. His pupils yawn back at me and I just huff and stare ahead too.

I can hear the TV on in Donna's room: an old movie, some ping-pong screwball dialogue. I wait for the silence that signifies a screen kiss. It doesn't come. More twittering. Then she changes channels – sounds like the news.

'Dean,' I say again.

He pays no attention. I tuck his hair behind his ears, but it slips back into his eyes again immediately. I wonder where his thoughts are. Is he listening to the TV too? Both just listening to the headlines, then. Both just inert. No anguish here, despite us being balled up together on the floor. I start thinking it would be nice to feel enough to shrink the world to this unkempt moonlit kitchen, to us two, to have everything pulling down this plughole.

Dean's so slightly built, but he feels heavy when, eventually, I put my hands in the corn-silk hair under his arms and pull him into my bedroom, watching his dragging feet in their hobo shoes bounce through the doorways.

In the morning he leans up on his elbows to look at me. We're both fully dressed in my narrow bed. He blinks through his fringe and says:

'Sorry about last night, Esther. You're lucky I

didn't start crying; that's what normally happens.'

Then he laughs. His silent laugh.

When we get up he doesn't act like he's got anywhere to go, so I take him to feed the birds in Heaton Park. From the gate by the station we walk down the cool, shaded slope to the pond. Where it curves to the right men are assembling tomorrow's funfair, bolting together the rusted, multicoloured pleasure apparatus. The mist is disappearing and a gluey, golden sunlight spreads instead. We lean on the railing and start tearing up bread. We have a whole stale loaf to throw.

Some Canada geese come and bob around and a swan wanders over, too. I start teasing it, waving a stiff slice at it then pulling it away to hide behind me. Its neck keeps dipping. Dean backs off.

'Hey, Esther, you want to be careful. It'll turn. You don't know what it's like to be pursued by an enormous angry flapping bird. It's not good.'

I turn to look at him. I squint against the sun. Dean shakes his head and looks very serious.

I say, 'Please, Dean, tell me you've been chased by a swan, it's perfect.'

He takes some bread off me, tears it up and drops it over the fence.

'Yes I have, and it wasn't funny.'

I can't stop smiling. I say, 'Well, what did you do to enrage it?'

'I don't remember. I was only small. I imagine I was probably poking it with a stick or something.'

Dean frowns then smiles. I smile too and then he nudges me in the ribs and pecks me with a kiss.

11

Donna thinks these developments with Dean are thoroughly hilarious, needless to say. She keeps shaking her head at me obscurely and playing that Simon and Garfunkel record with her bedroom door open. I saw Joey down Market Street last week and he started laughing before we'd even said hello. I stopped and put my hands in my hip pockets and glowered at him. I said:

'Don't laugh at me.'

He said, 'I'm not laughing at you, I'm laughing towards you.' He rolled his hands in my direction.

'How's your toy boy, Esther?' he said.

'Word gets around, doesn't it?' I said.

'He's a singer, isn't he?' he said.

I sighed. 'Oh probably. I mean yeah. I think he swapped his soul for some magic beans at a junction of the M62.'

Joey nodded. He said, 'The wolf at the door is after my magic beans.'

'Tell me about it,' I say. 'This is nothing, it's just silly. It's depressing really.'

'No, I think it's great. I'd never have picked you for a sex offender.'

More laughter. So, 'Bye Joey.' That was the end of that conversation.

Dean's good company, though, or he's diverting at any rate. I don't know. He's so viciously affectionate. You can't help but like that. His gnawed-at fingernails still manage to dig in my arm when he kisses me goodbye. He buys every book I mention. It's just that there's the sleepless, silent mornings, lying fully clothed with my back to him, my thin duvet oversoft and so cold it feels damp in the places where I stretch out my bare feet. Then I think we both lie staring. Or else I get up and go and sit in the kitchen. Anything to get away.

I've ignored his phone calls today. This evening Donna's giving me a lift up to Ancoats. She's off on some band business and I'm going to visit James, for some reason. She's wearing a Cossack hat with her jeans and T-shirt. I've got my thin Willa Cather dress on again, with bare legs and ballet shoes. When we get out of the car in the driving rain we shake hands to congratulate each other on our seasonal inappropriateness.

Weekday evenings usually find James brooding in his studio: a large room on the top floor of the Beehive Mill: a converted warehouse full of artists' spaces, practice rooms, creative cells. Dean's been seen round here. Donna's band rehearse in a room facing the cobbled courtyard. James's has a more exalting prospect. I have to take the creaking service lift to reach it. I sign in under Donna's name and walk past squashed boxes of flyers that are spilling their contents under the steep metal staircases. I heft the lift's lattice door, and then walk along to the end of the corridor on the top floor. The fire doors are all held open by heavy red fire extinguishers, so the bands can get their equipment in and out.

James pretends not to be pleased to see me. He opens the door a long time after I knock and he walks back inside without saying hello. He sits down at his paint-splattered table, with his shoulders rounded and his head on one side. I stand by the open window. The room smells of dust and fresh rain. Time was we used to watch storms from up here, billowing around the building, glowering at us two inside together with our tea. He would put pictures and messages up in the window for me to see when I was out walking. Today the clouds lie in rubble above the low, broken skyline; they smoke over the horizon as the sun sets there. I look round at James. He seems tired. No, his eyes look strangely smoky. I walk over and lean down in close to say:

'You wearing make-up, James?'

'Yeah, we've been doing some filming for this project . . .'

He shrugs and rubs at an eyebrow, not embarrassed like I want him to be.

'I wasn't implying that you were a transvestite necessarily,' I say. 'I was just noticing.'

He looks lost in thought, then he looks at me.

'Noticing is a great word, isn't it?' he says and smiles oddly.

'What else are you working on these days?' I say.

He looks stern and sighs, then he rifles the papers on the table and hands me some abstract charcoal sketches. 'I'm trying to do as many different things as I can. It seems like the better you are at one thing the more things you can't do. I have this idea . . .'

I watch as he brings the blade of his scored and paint-stained hand down diagonally between

162

us again and again, explaining. Saying 'the line',
'the body'.

I smile and nod.

'Yes, okay, what else?' I give the pictures back.
'And this.'

He moves some paper on the table and finds
a fat red scrapbook. It isn't even trying to close;
it sits on his knees concertina-ing.

'I'm quite into this at the moment,' he says.

He lets the book fall open where it wants to.
On a page full of tiny fruit labels: there must
be a hundred of them in neat columns and rows.

'No one pays attention to these,' he says, 'but
I like the colours.'

'I don't get it,' I say. He shrugs.

'So, what are you writing these days?' he asks,
twisting his head to a stupid angle to look out
of the window.

'Oh, same old same old: short stories about
sailors, convicts, cowboys, nuns. And my adventures in America. And this bloke I was in love
with the other week.'

Now he looks out of the window sceptically.

'Why shouldn't that be true?' I say. 'Anything's
true.'

He says, 'Why is it love, Esther? Why call it
that?'

'Because. Why is what you do art? Because you say so.'

'I don't say so.'

He doesn't, it's true. Checkmate.

I walk around the room looking at his things. His wizard's hat and a dusty cape are hanging on a curly old coat rack. He has a kettle on a tray and one sturdy mug upside down on the draining board next to a sink which has chalky paint swirling round the plughole. I unscrew the bottle of gin I've got in my satchel, take my plastic curly straw out of my ponytail and start drinking.

James rolls his eyes and does his best scornful sigh. He shakes his head.

'You're so in love with your lifestyle these days,' he says. I'm outraged.

'I don't have a lifestyle,' I say and drink more.

He leans back in his seat. He looks at me and says, 'Are you going back to the States?'

I frown at him. 'I never went to America, James.'

He really seems surprised. That's encouraging. He frowns at the table then looks up.

'Does Donna know this?'

'Course she does.'

'Course she does,' he says. He shakes his head again. He's always doing that. 'Where were you?'

164

'I wasn't anywhere.'

'You were here?'

'No. I didn't say that.'

'Oh, Esther. What are you going to do now then?'

I narrow my eyes at him. 'Same as ever. Walking and thinking. The days are about the feet, the nights are about the mind. That's my old epithet. I'll make a reading list. Actually, I think that's the plan for the whole rest of my life.'

'You believe in your plans, that's good,' he says. 'Then what?'

'What?' I say, and suck in some more warm gin.

'One day you're going to die,' he says.

'Stop blinding me with science,' I say. 'Stop jousting with me, Jimmy. Come and give me a hug. I'm lonely.' I say that in a singsong voice: I'm-Lone-ly. I'm-*Lone*-ly.

James doesn't move. James is unmoved.

'Those days are gone,' he says and smiles.

I tut. I slide my sticky straw back into my ponytail and smile back.

When I'm outside again I look up and shake a fist at his empty window. I say, 'Grrrrrrr.' With no conviction. Still, fruit labels. At least I can get drunk and sing songs with my friend.

I walk a lilting walk: my satchel bounces, my steps go tock-swish as I drop one foot in the gutter and swing it over the damp gravel there. Lampposts and spindly trees stand sentry in the small and empty car parks. Weeds fringe the streets. When the wind comes it bends the flowerless foxgloves.

I hopscotch on the bluish tarmac and the patched-up pavements. I'm singing a country song to the soaring unadorned warehouse walls which rise on either side of the thin streets. Here it is all sheer faces and awesome angles and windless, mossy, cobbled canyons. Everywhere is TO LET. A calm orange light touches the shattered windows: those toothed with grey jagged glass, those bricked up with grey breezeblocks or boarded with painted plywood or brittle rotting planks.

I reach the canal. The water is dark, flat and still with all the sludge on the surface pulled into marbled swirls and patterns by the lock gate. A taxi passes, slow and sinister, then a speeding old Escort with some kid shouting from the window. I walk and watch the sky not change. I smoke my invisible cigarette and keep on singing to myself. There are no other people around. Or wait, way over there in the rubble by that empty factory, a band on a photo shoot. That girl takes off her glasses and rubs one eye. The back line look away. Click.

12

Dean's sitting on a stool in the window of the coffee shop across the way there, shaking a sugar sachet and frowning at it. He's waiting for me. One of his shoes is half off, just hooked on his big toe. He's been swinging it back and forth against the footrail. I cross the road and go and knock on the glass in front of him. He looks startled, then his eyes light up.

We walk for a while, then sit by the fountains in front of the Town Hall. He presses his forehead against mine. I stay still with my eyes shut, feeling the low wind pull my hair, my dress, the ribbon in my plait all one way. I let my mind blank and feel his cold, slim hands on my neck and his kisses that are just dabs and swipes. When the rain starts getting noisy I lean back and look around, at the water making tiny glassy sculptures on the cobbles, in the puddles, on the cab roofs. The sky is low and dark. We stay where we are with rain streaming down our faces.

Later we walk along the canal under Whitworth Street. We sit down on a moss-slathered bench on the towpath. He starts talking about sex, of all things. Teenagers.

He says, 'Look, from things you've said to me it sounds as if people haven't been as careful as they might with you. Well, I'm just saying that I would be. What are you thinking?'

I'm reading the grafitti on the bench, fitting my thumbnail in the lines of the runic romances. I don't look up.

'What am I thinking? I'm thinking if we have this conversation we'll never be able to – have sex with each other.'

I look at him now. He shrugs when he says this:

'We will, Esther, because it's just mechanical.'

Oh, Jesus, he's wiser than I thought. He starts picking at the laddered knees of his pale jeans, twisting the bobbled grey string that stretches across his milky knees. His hair is covering his face up.

I get up and walk back towards the steps in silence. He catches up and walks alongside. There's flat silver light in the puddles he's sloping through but I'm cold now and I just want to go and sit in the pictures without him. I'm about to tell him that when he stops walking and folds his arms.

'Hey, Esther,' he says. 'I'm in love with you.' He won't look away.

'No you're not, Dean, stop being soft.'

'I am. I'm in love with you. Very much so.' He smiles very briefly and shows his tiny teeth.

'Calm down, junior,' I say and shake my head and walk off laughing. He calls after me.

'Don't call me junior. Hey, listen, if you don't say that you believe me I'm going to do something rash.'

I shrug without turning round. Then I do turn round, in time to see his shoes land under the bench where he's thrown them, and then him falling backwards into the canal. His denim legs and anoraked arms flourish in a bunch for a split second before he goes under. His hair lifts into thick fluff and then he's bobbing there in the scummy water with it pasted down his cheeks, looking very pleased with himself.

He beams at me and stretches his arms out to swim.

Donna calls it the deed of darkness. When it comes to it, as it was bound to, I suppose, I turn away and curl up, stay dead still, looking at the shadows on my cardboard boxes and thinking about nothing. Dean's huffing breath is on my bare shoulder. He moves his hand over the stubble on my shins, spreads his slim calloused fingers on my stomach then moves his hand up. He whispers.

'Turn around, Esther,' he says.

It takes me a while to do that. And when I do, I feel nothing at all, in any part of myself. I don't feel bad but I do feel nothing. So while he has his head in my neck, kissing me, I take a handful of his slippy blond hair and keep him there while I swirl some thick spit around my mouth, spoon it up with my tongue, claw it out with three fingers of my free hand and make like I'm fiddling with myself so I can rub it on. That could feel bleak if I let it. But then he slides himself along me, lifts his head up, stares through his fringe and says:

'Esther! Isn't skin great?'

That makes me feel less gloomy. It makes me giggle, actually. I can look at his face and like him a lot. He's a great kid, a good person. But when I look down at the squash of my thighs against his lean, slippy stomach I just feel dread. I wonder if he can tell. I put my hand flat where his heart would sound, is sounding, and then wish I hadn't in case he does it back to me. I don't want to make him feel bad. But this isn't going to happen again.

So I don't call him or answer when he calls me. I'd been getting on with my work for a week or so when he just started showing up here after he'd been at the bar. I can't really turn him away. He leans on our buzzer at 3 a.m. If I'm not awake Donna bangs on the wall by my bed. Then the sharp noise pulls me along the fuzzy hallway to let him in. I stand at the top of the stairs and he comes crashing up with something in his eyes that says he isn't as drunk as he's acting. He says:

'This is what happens when you take in a stray,'

or

'Oh my God, an attractive boy has come round to see you. What a pain.'

Even when I've been horrible to him, he still smiles when he shows up: he's always unfazed. Last night we were in bed and he took a Biro from the mug on my dresser and drew daisy chains around my wrists while I was reading. No mean feat, so I put the book down and took the pen to make a spindly anchor inside his forearm. The blue scrawl on his pale skin looked like neon left on in daylight. I pressed a thumb along the thin blue watercolour strokes inside his wrists. I said to him:

'Is this what eighteen-year-olds do then?'

He stopped still and shook his fringe.

'No, Esther, don't say things like that. This is what me and you do.'

'Right,' I said.

But it is a regular adolescent love-in, us pretending to be so endlessly fascinated with each other. While Dean's asleep he twitches and talks. He rubs his child legs together like tinder. His arms grip my middle or my neck or he just holds my hand if that's all that's available. At first light today I untangle myself, sit up and push out the window to escape the sour air in here, to try and forget that he's in that unfamiliar bed behind me, awake now and watching me.

I slide off the bed to sit in front of the unframed mirror that leans against the wall. I get my make-up from my satchel, mascara my eyes and then tip my red, butterfly-shaped perfume bottle on to my neck, letting my dirty hair fall slow, in a piece, as I spread the oily pools behind my ears. I put some on my wrists too and the Biro there dissolves. I get back in bed without looking at Dean. He puts a hand on the lumpy skin on the outside of my thigh and presses his chin down on all the plughole knots on top of my head. I close my eyes and let the dull morning bloom there, trying to think of somewhere else or the future or the past. Then he turns me around and there's a soft pinch and press on my eyelids one by one, and his nothing breath on my forehead, his cold radiator ribcage against me.

I look out of the window as usual to watch him go. I wonder what I'm playing at. I should feel grimmer about this than I do. He stops at the gate and looks back at me, he beams at me, thumps his heart with his hand before tripping off somewhere. His shoulders always seem to be twitching, like he's arguing with himself in his mind.

'Has he been swiping you with his kiss curl?' Donna asks from the doorway.

It's a tricky one. I like having Dean's arm around me on the bus sometimes, but I find myself biting back tears when he's moving in me. And I've told him, more than once, don't come round anymore, I'm busy. But he still comes round, and I still let him in. Today he told me he'd written a song about me.

'Sing it for me, sweetheart,' I said. 'I'll look into your eyes the whole time you do . . .'

He didn't resent the sarcasm because he didn't notice it. No, that's not true. It simply didn't occur to him that I'd be that nasty. He tells me he loves me all the time. Once he said:

'If you're in*sane*. And you *find* someone. You should *move*, and *fast*.'

He's quite right. But I don't take it seriously. He doesn't know the first thing about me. Then again: what's to know? I've been writing a lot of things down recently about being a nothing-person. I try to talk to him about it.

We're sitting next to each other on my bed, both drunk, both slumped back so far we're almost sliding on to the floor. He's declaring himself again and I'm listening to the dawn chorus. It's just making me lonely. Lonely, exhausted, resentful. I turn and ask him what can he so love and adore about me when I never say anything I mean; when there's nothing I can definitively say to him about anything. I'm *nothing*, I tell him.

'You've just been drawn into a vacuum,' I say. 'There's nothing here. Honestly.'

'When someone you care about says that you worry,' he says. He frowns.

I say, 'Well you're demonstrating my point now. Because what I'm saying is just bad rhetoric, just spiel. And you're buying it. This is exhausting me. We're having a conversation about nothing.'

It feels like he's pushing over plywood fronts; they float back into dust, they're falling with no sound. And there's nothing behind. I'm a nothing-person. So I'm not sure how things would work. I mean, what do people do who are nothing-people? It's just my narcissistic introspection is drawing him in, like a black hole, a concentrate of nothingness, a maze of mirrors . . .

'You're such a pain, Esther,' he says, rolling his eyes, touching the top of my arm and shaking his head. Then he sits up straight and says, 'Hey, Esther, I've been thinking, you've got to promise never to put me in one of your stories.'

'Oh, I won't,' I say and then he's quiet. He rubs at the spots on his chin, shakes his fringe.

'Why did you have to say it like that?' he says. 'You're such a pain.'

Not that it matters a damn, but I don't like what I'm doing. I keep telling him I'm busy and it's true, I am busy, but again and again now I find myself going into town late to get him. I think

I'm addicted to someone being pleased to see me. To that moment when he looks up from the book he's reading at the till on the door and really smiles. I think about that look as I'm walking up Oldham Street to the bar, past the dog at the bus stop and the screaming matches outside the clubs. I know I look borderline cadaverous: frizzed, chapped, blurring round the edges from the drink. Dean doesn't mind. His face lights up.

Or at least it did. One night last week when I walked in and winked at him he just twitched a polite smile and went back to his book. His eyes were blank. So I had to keep walking and go and talk to Barbara Ann at the bar instead. I felt sick. She was nice about it, maybe she didn't see. She invited me to her birthday party. I won't go, but I said, 'Sounds good.'

'Yeah,' she said, smiling, 'and Dean's coming, too.'

But Dean's not been answering my calls since, either, the calls I make, jabbing at him in the middle of my sleepless nights. I tell Donna about it. She's sitting on her bed, hunched up tiny, bending notes on her guitar.

'He's proving immune to my powers of desperation, it's very irritating,' I say. I've got my arms folded and I don't know what to do with myself.

'Aren't boys funny,' she says, keeps playing.

I go back to my room and lock all the locks. I get into bed early and lie listening to my stomach creaking and my eyelashes grazing the pillow. When Donna knocks on to see if I'm coming out for karaoke I don't reply. I roll over to lie on my back with my hands crossed on my chest. My taped-up box towers look stately in the moonlight. My clothes and records are all tidied away again, too: there's no clutter, no personality, just grey light on flat surfaces.

I don't know what I'm pushing for when I get myself worked up. My mind seems to be a tirelessly elastic web, where everything is accommodated, worse than accommodated. It's unbreachable, I've decided. Things struggle and are stuck there: ideas strung up as lightless lanterns, people just weightless, faceless blackened husks.

Example: there was this girl Helen I had a bombastic friendship with a couple of years back. She was a broad-beamed Geordie I met when I was working in the bar. We knocked about together for a few months, went to the theatre together. She was an old-fashioned English student with windswept ideals. The last lines of any Fitzgerald book made her shake her head and cry. Quite right, too. Her and Richard had a conversation about him once. Richard thought he had an angle, that he understood. Helen pulled on her plait and rolled her eyes. She said, 'Can I suggest that *you don't?*' Over and over. I was impressed; she was double obnoxious. Richard hated her, called her a stupid fat bitch. Not to her face, of course. He probably wanted to slap her. Slap her and fuck her both, that's the way it works with these people, isn't it? He hated me having any friends. He hated Donna and she thought he was hilarious. To start with she thought he was hilarious.

Anyway, Helen. We used to talk and talk until our spit was thick, not the way it is with Donna at all. But when she finished her course she started acting cowardly about life and I found I couldn't be around it. I couldn't talk about things with her when her face always looked scared: her eyes big and her mouth tiny. Her laugh got louder and meant less. I left her standing at a bus stop one day, looking like a drudge with her shopping bags, and her change purse jammed under her armpit. She was fading out, I thought. In fact she was literally fading out: all dressed in baby colours: pale blue jeans and a yellow coat. Summer pastels. So timid, so cowed. She'd left the path. She came in to the bar one night and I halfway told her why we couldn't hang out anymore. I saw the dark colour spreading on to her chin, forehead, her neck and her nose. I was attacking her because I was too scared to help her. I looked down. I licked a finger and turned a page. It's always been the way. People who seem to be cowards or martyrs bring out the ugliest feelings in me: blasts of scorn which I can feel flashing in my eyes. I think they're being cheap with their lives, that's why. So they seem ravenous for the worst thoughts I can have. That's why I was the way I was with Mum, too. I'm not making excuses, I'm being honest. Now I look round this bare room, and feel sick with myself for the way I was to her just because she wanted friendly, familiar things around her. Because, God knows, me and my brother were neither of those things. She grew us in her stomach then we ate her alive. I can't start thinking about that time. Besides she's okay now, isn't she?

Truth be told I don't really think of Mum or Helen as being out there now feeling happy or unhappy or otherwise. When – if – those people reappear I think, Oh, are they still about? and that's all I think. Sometimes something happens to me and I think the same about myself: Ah, Esther, what has she been up to all this time, I wonder? I don't really wonder. I don't care. I'm a clown, I'm a ghoul, I barely exist. I try hard not to exist, to write and be that instead.

But then there are nights like tonight, when thinking of that first uncertain kiss has my mouth gluey and my heart hot. Why do I feel that if I don't exist? Why do memories crowd in? Of old humiliations giving me this feeling of maggots in my stomach. Of my violent tempers, like ice in my veins. And the loneliness, the fingers clawing blindly inside.

I woke up here once recently, in the very early hours, and it took a moment to register, to work out what was different. There were warm arms around me, the tickle of knees tucked in behind mine, someone breathing on my shoulder. A memory, a wish, a phantom? I didn't dare move. I was awake and staring in the darkness and I could still feel it. It was so real. But it wasn't real. I lie back now with my eyes in the crook of my arm, listen to the dripping windowsill and try to not think about anything.

13

I decide to trek out to Barbara Ann's party, after all. All the way to Chorlton at 1 a.m. on the off-chance of seeing Dean's not very friendly face. Very dignified, Esther.

I swing myself up and shake my fuzzy head, sit on the edge of my bed feeling sick at myself, and feeling grubby. I find I can roll up plastic dirt on my hands, but the flat feels too cold now to get undressed and have a bath. I keep shivering. Shuddering actually. I lick my creaking teeth and shudder. I push back my cardigan sleeve and look at the blonde hairs standing up austerely there, stiff amongst the scars and the white bumps of a couple of flea bites. I blow on them and they barely move. All I want to do is curl up on top of the soft, smudged duvet, just for ten minutes, albeit with my dress pinching and my cardigan itching. I couldn't cry now. I could make the noises but my throat would just ache, my stomach would cringe tighter and tighter, I know how it would feel. I've no time for this. The red numbers keep changing: 1.15 now. I stand up and my skin feels tight and tender. I loop my key ring around one finger and go out.

I set off for town, looking out for a taxi. My body tenses against the breeze. My bare legs tingle. My shoulders are squeezed up in my cardigan, my hands balled and then stretching, my steps small and fast, heels thudding dully on the pavement. In my pocket I'm playing with my keys, twirling the ring round my finger. It falls off more than once, and they make a sound like smashing china when they hit the ground.

The house is a big lit-up semi at the end of a long, dark street. I go in by the back door, to the crowded kitchen to find a drink. There isn't much left. I empty the dregs of a bottle of vodka into a plastic cup. There's a scruffy girl sitting up on the counter, in an old jumper and a cut-off black cord skirt. Her ink-stained fingers grip the neck of a bottle of red wine she keeps swigging. A tall, dark-haired man by the fridge is leaning forward to talk to her, to breathe on her: his face seems on the brink of something, it's frightening and hysterical when he laughs without humour in the strip light. She yawns.

Her teeth are blue. She jumps down from her Formica perch and takes a CD from her satchel. The cover shows a doorway. I recognise it. She heads out into the hall, waving the fingers of one hand at him – goodbye – after she's turned away. I follow her out. In the hallway we stand aside for Barbara Ann, who's wheeling along on an orange Chopper bike. It looks new, it has a carnival of corkscrewing white ribbons on the handlebars. She's beaming.

'Check it out, Esther, it's off my brother,' she says, and pauses to pull on her glossy blue-black topknot. 'Yeah, it's Game Over for me – I'm going straight back to childhood.'

She pedals on into the kitchen. A string of admirers follow.

I look in the back room for Dean. No joy there, and he isn't smoking in the front room either. Then I notice him. He's sitting scowling on the stairs: his chin's on his chest and his arms are folded. He must know I'm here. People keep tutting when they have to climb up and down past him. Sometimes those people are in pairs, are holding hands. Romance.

I lean back against the front door and look at him. He stares meaningfully at me through the banisters for half a moment, then he lifts his eyes away. I can't have that. I pour some white wine in my cup from a bottle on the sideboard, then go and sit next to him. He bumps down to the step below and so I slide down next to him. Now he bumps down two steps and huffs. Silly kid. I want him to look at me. I finish my drink and balance the weightless plastic beaker on my head. I look into the warm darkness of the back room. Dark except for a swarm of dancing cigarettes, the little bars on the stereo and a burping lava lamp. The girl on the couch closes her eyes to listen to the slow tune she's put on. She's somewhere else now. Well, Lord love this noble group. We're all sincere people. I look at Dean sitting next to me, staring at a corner of the dim hallway, sucking on a switch of his hair. Somehow I'm crying out inside for him to look at me. I think I can't take another second if he doesn't. He takes the beaker off my head and puts it on his own and then I nudge him gently in the ribs with my elbow and it falls off. I say, 'You okay, Dean?'

He still doesn't look at me.

He says: 'Esther, I've been thinking. Why do you think it's impossible that someone might actually like you?'

There's a question. I roll my eyes.

'I don't,' I say, 'I'm probably too fond of myself, if anything.'

'You know next time you feel down I'll come round with a feather and tickle you. I'll come round with a Beach Boys record and I'll pull you off the bed and twirl you round the room.'

He brings his fist down on his knee for emphasis. I look at the ceiling and huff.

'What the fuck is up with you?' he says. He means it too.

'I'm sorry. You know, I'm a redhead. I'm supposed to have a temper.'

Dean looks confused. He says, 'What – do you dye it brown?'

'What are you talking about. My hair is red.'

'Auburn maybe. In the sun.'

'It's damn well red. Fuck you.'

'Hey, Esther, you're so touchy today.'

'Well, I don't understand why you'd say that about me, that's all.'

'I've touched a nerve, that's why you're getting upset,' he says.

'No.' I shake my head again and cough out a failed laugh. My voice sounds high and thin. 'I'm getting upset because I know you're never going to touch a nerve with me,' I say.

'Oh God,' he says. 'Is this about that note you

carry around and stick up on your mirror every night. This someone you knew for two days, and you'll never see again. Give me a break.'

'I'm not going to explain that to you,' I tell him. 'It would be pointless. That was . . . ,' I shrug. 'That was . . . '

'I see,' he says, and looks down at his hands on his knees. He nods to himself and says, 'So that's why you didn't think it was significant about the birthdays.'

'I guess so,' I say.

He's silent for a little while. Then he smiles and sighs and changes the subject. He tells me he's got his own room these days, in a house in Whalley Range.

'Well, that's good news, Dean. How's it working out?' I say.

'Yeah, it's a shoebox with mouldy walls, but it's very nice to be able to lay my stuff out, play some records. It's made me realise that if I ever get my own flat it's going to look just great. Cluttered.'

He smiles and nods again and so do I. My name's all smashed up when he says it next and puts an awkward arm around me. He's wearing an old jumper, the wool feels soft on my back. I look up and then down again.

'Sorry, Dean,' I say. He takes his arm away, claps once, then shakes his head and stands up: leaves without looking at me again. Good for him.

I decide to sit the party out until morning. I pour some more nasty wine and go and curl up on an armchair in the stale-smelling, curtain-free front room. I pull someone's damp duffel coat over me and squeeze myself up so my knees are by my chin. I close my eyes but don't sleep. The music and the smoking go on and on. I think about my bedroom. After a few shivery hours the sun starts coming up and the street-lights switch off.

The coat's gone. I don't remember that happening. I stand up and wince as I stretch. My legs are heavy liquid and I feel like there's some coarse random corsetry pulling my back muscles tight. This room is icy, above the ankle-high body-heat of the three people I don't know asleep on the floor.

Standing at the bus stop to go into town the skin on my arms feels stiff and sore. So the calendar says it's summer: it's damn cold. When I get off in Piccadilly the sky is a glaring pale grey and feels very low. It hurts to look up, it sets me on edge. I keep my eyes on the pavement, while I'm walking, sometimes even lift a hand to shade them. I stagger down a deserted Mosley Street to Saint Peter's Square, doing Donna's alien robot walk on and off, walking over the silver light in the pavement puddles. I lift up my dress and see how the cold is bringing out mauve and orange shapes on my knees.

All the municipal street furniture, the bins and bollards, the flower-filled troughs and the lamp-posts, have worker bees painted on them in gold. I lean against a cold stone wall and copy one into my detective notebook, carefully shading in the wings. I walk on through the silence which is deepened by the distant thrum of traffic on the flyovers, laced with the birdsong which rises and falls in the potted trees to each side and ahead. It's not raining at the moment but wind is shaking water off those trees every which way.

I lie down in the garden which dips in front of Central Library and take my letter from my wallet to read. It's soft and splitting along the creases now. A dissolving treasure map. An obsolete treasure map that I'm still carrying around:

Dearest Esther,
My name is Newton, and as alarming as this may sound — well, you left me in your bed this morning.

Trust me, I should know, I just woke up here. I do recall some charming young woman loafing around, fiddling with her red hair, drinking tea, acting both calm and quite nervous all at once (??) . . . Hmmm . . . I guess I'm hoping that was you. Suffice to say, being in an absolute stranger's apartment I quickly tied a blindfold around my eyes to keep from seeing anything too incriminatingly personal. It was actually just a sock I found and I think I have porcelain in my foot from attempting to locate the toilet. Damn. But honestly – I'll see you this evening and, I hope, we can work these odd events of leisure out.

Love, Newton.

xxxxxx

We failed there didn't we? I did. You think I'm being a coward not ringing him. So much time has dripped by. I should just bite the Biro and call. Because if I make that effort just imagine how the world could open up, finally, finally, my sodden life burst into flames, and all my mean spirits burn away for good. I should do that. It's not like I ever pretended to have any self control. But.

'Esther, aren't you lonely?' Dean asked me last night.

I told him, 'This world has enough fevered

egos on the loose without me letting mine out there on some ravenous love quest.'

Now why did I say that? It does sound ridiculous. But I believe it all the same.

Dawn stretches in the clouded sky while the dew soaks through my dress. I try to relax and not shiver. If only I could get that under control then I feel like I could stay here a long time, watching the days leaking into the nights, swilling over the buildings, bleeding back again. I could lie and not think of anything but ways to describe the sky, the clouds, the light.

14

When I got home from the pictures today
Dean was sitting folded up on the stairs outside
our front door. I didn't want to see the look
in his eyes, so I raised a hand to shield myself,
and I didn't look up as I fiddled with the damn
lock. He tore a page off one of the take-out
menus by the postboxes, balled it up and threw
it. It hit my leg. I ignored it and he started
talking, every word sounding so considered
and huffed over, every breath sounding
snatched.

'Okay, Esther, I want to say that I'm sorry I
was so intense and that it's only because I was
really unhappy when we met, you know, don't
want to talk about that. So I was acting insane,
I mean you're insane too, so it's okay, but
nonetheless, I shouldn't have jumped in the canal
or sworn at those old men.'

I ignored him. I didn't say what I almost said:
that he must *never be sorry, never be unhappy*. I

couldn't even do that. I kept my hand up so I wasn't looking at him.

And now the dark is thick and the only noise in this bedroom is the swish of the needle round a record that's been over forever. The truth comes out at times like this.

When I woke up with Newton here I remember surprising myself with this simple thought, that *Something's changed in me that can't change back.* I really hoped so. But now I lie dead still on my back and click my eyes from corner to corner of the ceiling: down and across, up and across the dim white rectangle of artex stippling. My mind clicks too, into this limping mantra of self-serving humility: *I'm not a cynic. I'm not an egomaniac. I'm trying hard at my work.* I doubt if any of those things are true. But I say them over and over, frowning at the ceiling.

Donna knocks on my door when she gets home. I don't answer but she comes in and sits on the end of the bed, in the dusty slice of golden light falling in from the hallway.

'Hey, Esther,' she says.

'I'm fine,' I say.

'You're not fine.'

'I'm turning into an opera, but I'm fine.'

'No, you're turning into a George Jones song. But that's not so bad.'

I want to stay still but my mouth turns down and my legs pull up. Donna lies down on the covers behind me. We say what we used to say when we were kids. I nod against the pillow.

'Come in the kitchen and we'll talk about this,' she says. 'Wait while I get the biscuits from my room.'

'Biscuits,' I say and nod again and then get up and follow her out. She's made a pot of tea already. I sit down. I collect my fists on the table and then turn my hands over and spread them to watch the stitched welts: grey turning red. I breathe out slowly. Donna's going to help me.

But it gets me first, and I know what I'm going to do. I stand up and pick up the teapot, transfer it to my left hand, cradle its scalding weight there for one nice second before hurling it at the wall. It smashes and sharp pieces bounce back my way. The wallpaper steams where it's stained. Donna comes back and reaches up to pretend strangle me.

'Stop wrecking the joint, soft girl. Sit down. Come on, Esther, we'll talk about it. It's okay. Sit. Wait. Tea's off then. Sit while I get that brandy I hid from you last week.'

She comes back from the bedroom with the alcohol and pours out drinks for us both.

'I'm sorry, Donna. I just get in such a fugitive temper, sometimes,' I say, and lift my mug up but don't drink. 'I work myself into an operatic pitch of emotion, and I teeter there feeling I don't know what and then I just slide back down the scale with helpless dopiness on my face. Feel nothing again. It exhausts the hell out of me. But I can't be without it. You don't have that, do you?' I say. I drink some brandy.

She puts her head on one side and says, 'Well, no. I do my own thing, say my piece and amuse myself, and no one ever treads on anyone's toes. But that's just me.'

'I think you've got the right idea, Donna. I don't know what I'm playing at. I feel so romantic and furious all the bloody time.'

She frowns. I go on.

'I have this monstrous self-pity in me and this monstrous self-love, I keep making my lip tremble. I keep starting sentences in my mind with "My whole life . . .", "All my life . . ."'

'That's not so terrible,' Donna says. 'I'd like to feel those things sometimes but I don't or I can't. You believe in the green light,' she says, 'and I think that's great.'

'Yes I do,' I say. 'The New World.'

'White socks,' she says. She twitches a smile.

'. . . And one fine morning –'

'Of course. In the meantime stop smashing all the crockery up. We'll be eating out of pans and drinking out of . . .'

'Pineapples.'

'Heaven forfend.'

She pours more brandy in my mug.

'Do you want to do some dancing?' she says.

I shrug and have some drink. She leans over me to the machine and pushes play. There's a whirring but no music yet.

'Romantic and furious,' she says. 'How the bloody hell else do you want to feel anyway?'

'I've been missing . . . you know,' I say.

She nods. 'I know,' she says. 'But you just have to . . .'

She frowns and squints up one eye, says, 'hmmm . . .'

I say, 'I have to . . . burst out of the cold bath. I have to run downstairs in my widow's weeds.'

Donna slaps her hands on her cheeks and sticks out her tongue: pulls a gargoyle face. I do one back.

So I'm taking my notebook on a trip. I've been

sitting in this café on the station concourse watching a cup of tea get cold. Now I slide my Biro out from my ponytail and smoke it as I walk to my platform. A light rain blows indoors and I can see weeds waving under the bridge.

My train skates through scarred expanses of sickly looking grass. A pair of wine-coloured carriages thud past on the other line. By the concrete chimneys at a chemical plant, another set sits stalled. Scribbled lines of trees span the flat fields, their clutching twigs shiver. The wind is slicing all around.

I reach the coast at last and follow signs down a narrow, slaloming street to the front. It just keeps getting colder. On a bench facing out, two old ladies sit sucking fudge and agreeing with each other about something endlessly.

The vistas here are all grey: barely differentiated strata of water, land, sky. I hug myself as I walk along the sharp, pebbled beach, thinking maybe I should go and touch the sea, since I crossed so much country to get here, but I don't, I just look out and concentrate. My skin tightens into gooseflesh and my eyes sting. There's all sorts washed up here, now I look around, an array of sand-scabbed souvenirs: empty bottles, snatches of frayed rope, seashells that look like snapped fingernails. I kneel down, take some paper I've written on from my wallet and tear it up. In a shallow pool, swelling in the disturbed water, I've watched it slowly, slowly turn to pulp.